Dream On

by Jonathan Moch

ISBN-13: 978-0-9815299-4-3

Table of Contents

Chapter 1

The House Was Quiet and the World Was Calm.

The hardest part of living is death. Not something we generally think about until someone we love moves on to the perfect wave in the sky.

When a member of the surf community dies, their loved ones throw them a paddle out, a surfer's version of a funeral. Traditionally we paddle out beyond the deceased's favorite surf break, arranging ourselves in a circle. Leis and flowers are tossed into the middle. Then we say something about the person who died, and we give silent prayers as someone spreads the ashes.

Sitting on my surfboard, amidst this raw beauty, I thought about what I would say. On the horizon, the stars and moon peeked their way in just above the yellow and pink sky of the sun's last crest at the ocean's edge. I set the lei upon the water, careful not to drop the urn. It was requested by the family for me to be the final voice after a moment of silent prayer and then spread the ashes.

I can't help but celebrate the life we had, rather than focusing on our loss. People shy away from telling you about suffering and hard trials. Instead, they wait until you're blindsided by them. And although we don't enjoy suffering, we shouldn't fear it, but embrace it like a big wave. Surfing's a lot like life. They're both a sea of minefields full of sharks, riptides, and other unknowns demanding the acceptance of chaos. It's embracing the chaos that makes it wonderful.

We always called ourselves the four musketeers, but now we were down to three. The name stuck, because Tommy, Jessie, and Lee were friends long before I came into the picture. After the summer of 1985, we had a bond of friendship that was hard to explain.

Before I got to know them, I was afraid of anything even remotely close to chaos. Everything seemed totally impossible and I felt like life had dealt me a bad hand.

I was thirteen, late in the spring of 1985. I had tested out of 8th grade, so on to a new school. And now fitting in would be even harder. I was living in a small Orange County suburb of over 2 million people, but to me, it was the loneliest place in the world.

Growing up, kids talk about their dreams — everything from being a famous athlete to going to the moon. My dream was to have everyone's approval, especially my dad's. He was a doctor, so I thought if I became a great doctor, then he would have to love me, and so would everyone else.

Truth be told, at that time, I longed to be anybody but me. I felt that everyone else had it better. I wanted to be the popular kid, the star athlete, or even be the toughest kid in school. Instead, I was that kid, the one everyone liked to pick on. And with a name like Benjamin Dover III, I was a prime target for being tortured by others. Especially when José Lòpez made life even more unbearable. The last time he caught me on the way home, I didn't think I'd live to see another day.

Two of his buddies were holding me. He looked at me, smiled, and hit me square in the face. And let me tell you, that freakin' hurts, and oh my gosh, it tears you up no matter what, which only encouraged these jackals even more. The blood from my nose hadn't yet reached my lips before he slugged me in the gut. Which, by the way, isn't pleasant either. At this point, his crew must have let go of me because I remember doubling up into a ball and hitting the ground.

All I could smell was like this metallic iron scent, my vision was blurred, and breathing hurt so bad. This was when things got a little fuzzy, and all I could remember was all of them kicking me while I asked God to please let me die. Then I heard one kid say, "Pick him back up."

"No, kick the weddo." Another shouted.

I was hoisted back to my feet, barely able to stand. There I was, face to face with José Lòpez. He slapped me in the face and said, "No teachers to save your ass this time, so why don't you just BenDover," José said. He had such bad breath and always got in my face.

Out of the corner of my eye I saw a figure emerge from the shadows. "Leave him alone!" shouted Lee.

Lee had just been released out of Juvenile Hall. I really didn't know him at the time, but there he was like the knights of old. He could have easily been one of those guys you see in surf magazines, ripped and dressed way cool. Lee was shorter than most but tough as nails. He didn't hang out with any of the other Latino kids at the school. In fact, only a hand full of people at school would even talk to him. One being this bleached blond Asian kid named Tommy, he was cool to everyone. He didn't seem to care that Lee went to

Juvie. Tommy, as a freshman, was a starting quarterback and lead the football team to a CIF championship. The only thing Tommy loved more than football was surfing.

Lee slid one of the straps of his backpack off, “I said, leave him alone.”

“Why? What’s he to you?” José looked at his buddies and back at Lee. He smiled, “You don’t scare me.” He turned and faced me again. His fist flew into me so hard it lifted me off the ground. I fell to the pavement in pain.

As I fell, I watched a bag full of books rocketed at one of the kids who kicked me earlier. It collided with his head with a loud thud sending him to the ground next to me.

Lee pulled a butterfly knife from his pocket. He flicked his wrist back and forth. The blade danced in his hands, and in seconds it was readied.

The kid on the ground ran away, crying, and the two other kids bolted as well, yelling, “He’s crazy!”

“You’re nothing without that,” José said, pointing at Lee’s knife.

Smiling, Lee folded it back up and put it away. José pulled a switchblade from his pocket and lunged it at Lee. Lee grabbed José’s wrist, jerked it back, dislodging the blade from his hand, jumped up and pounded José square in the face, breaking his nose. Blood splattered all over. José swung his fists frantically, unable to see. Lee ducked and rocketed his fist into Lòpez’s stomach, knocking the wind out of him.

José dropped to his knees. Lee grabbed the back of his head, wipped it back, and whispered in his ear, “Tell anyone, and I’ll kick your ass ten times worse.”

José held his stomach as he hobbled off defeated.

“You’re nothing,” Lee yelled at him.

I remember trying not to cry, but I am sure a few tears escaped as I thanked him. He nodded his head and helped me up. His books had fallen out of his bag. They looked like they had never even been cracked open. We picked them up together.

"I think this is the first time I ever used a book this year," he said.

He helped me up and dusted me off. We walked together through a field. I couldn't help wondering about his last statement.

"How did you pass math without ever opening the book?" I asked.

"I copied off you. That's why you always leaned to the left, right?"

"Oh yeah, of course," I said, knowing full well that I had no clue Lee had been cheating off me. And if I had known, I probably would have told on him.

He went on, "I always thought it was cool you didn't say anything and never even asked for a favor. Did me a real solid."

We continued walking together. He flipped open the red-topped box, popped out a cigarette, and slid it onto his lip. The zippo lighter he pulled out seemed so cool. The way it flipped open igniting the flame was so cinematic. He put the fire to his cigarette, took a few puffs, and relaxed.

He noticed me watching, smiled, pulled another cigarette, and offered it to me. I thanked him with a smile but gestured no thanks. He put it away, with no offense taken by the refusal as we continued to walk together. He followed me all the way to my house and never said another word. I think I was wrong about Lee. Just cause he went to Juvie, doesn't automatically mean he's a terrible person, right?

I couldn't sleep that night, between the rain, and all that had happened. I walked to the other side of the house, to my parent's open bedroom door, but the bed was empty as usual. My mom and dad were both on call that night, and when the hospital pages, they have to go. It just would have been nice if they had let me know, but I guess that was the time I lived in.

I was part of that generation of latchkey kids who went through their all-important and formative years, as one of the least parented, least nurtured generations in U.S. history. A time when seat belts weren't required, cops let you off with a warning, and life was your own to figure out.

My parents were going to be in Europe for a few weeks that summer, lecturing. There was a debate on what to do with me. Dad insisted I'd be okay staying home alone, especially after my uncle abandoned me to go on a gambling bender the previous summer while they were gone. Mom, on the other hand, felt he should give my uncle another chance as somebody would be better than nobody.

I walked through the long open hallway to the main entrance to the house. Thinking about their debate as I passed by the massive, well-kept saltwater fish tank my dad had installed. I stared at it and looked around the room. The rain and the reflections on the walls made me appear to be like a fish in a tank myself.

I grabbed my favorite deck of cards and practiced some of the stuff Uncle John taught me last summer. Some people count sheep when they can't sleep, I found counting cards was way more relaxing. Plus, I had been working on a few new tricks all summer, and I had to perfect them. Everybody likes a good card trick, and since I knew I was socially inept, it was quite possibly the only way I would ever fit in.

I shuffled the deck a few times then lifted the top card. It was the ace of heats. I slid it back into the deck. The lionfish in the tank stared at me. I said to him, "Watch this," and threw the deck of cards at the fish tank. The cards hit and scattered in all directions. It was so cool to see how the water reflected light bounced off them. All the cards fell to the floor except one. The ace of hearts was stuck to the tank blocking the view of the lionfish. This was the first time I actually got the trick to work. And I have to say it was pretty cool.

Dream On

***

The next day my routine was the same. I sat watching everyone else with their friends as I sat alone at the lunch tables.

"Watz up!" Tommy announced. He plopped himself down right across from me at the table.

I was in shock, here was one of the most popular kids in school, and he was talking to me. Tommy sat there, waiting for a response. I could smell his Juicy Fruit bubble gum from across the table. I marveled at how, even when he talked, he never stopped chewing. How did he not bite off his tongue? He stared at me, waiting for a response. All I could utter was, "Um mm."

Jessie appeared out of nowhere, he was always wearing fighter jet t-shirts, but today he was wearing a Ronald Reagan shirt that read, the Gipper. He popped Tommy on the shoulder, saying, "Hey, scooch!"

"Chill," Tommy retorted. Tommy moved to the right.

Jessie plopped down next to him, shoving him a little more to the right.

Tommy looked at me and said, "Dude. Nice hand me down to Lòpez."

"Oh, I didn't—" I started, but was interrupted by Lee jumping into the seat next to me. He wrapped his arm around me and announced, "You should have seen this guy punk his ass."

"I always miss the good stuff," Jessie said.

Lee continued, "Dude here, popped that poser right in the nose."

"Sweet!" said Tommy.

I tried to interject, "That's not—"

Lee nudged me and motioned to Tommy, "That's Tommy."

Tommy flew a peace sign, and Jessie followed with, "Hey, didn't we play on the same—"

"Yes, we were on the Angels together," I said.

Tommy laughed at Jessie, "Like, you've ever been an angel."

Jessie ignored him and continued to interrogate me, "Why did you stop?" Before I could answer, he said to Tommy and Lee, "He had a wicked curve and was the best hitter in the league."

All eyes were on me. To be honest, I quit because I lost the first game of the championships that year and couldn't handle losing again. But I quickly came up with what I thought was an acceptable excuse, "Nobody listened to the coaches, and then I sprained my wrist. I didn't want to screw up my chances at med school."

"Damn dude, that's some long-term shit right there," Tommy said.

The school bell rang, and all the kids scattered like birds avoiding prey. Tommy looked around and laughed as if being late was no big deal to him, he looked back at us and said, "Lates! Hey, we still hanging this weekend?"

Lee, with a simple, "Dude." Followed by Jessie's "Cha."

I sat there, and again everyone was staring at me, I was dumbfounded and in shock until Lee elbowed me, and I replied, "Oh, I'd love to."

Tommy laughed and, with a loud pitch, announced, "Sike! I'm bumming it this weekend with my cuz at the beach, you're on your own. Lates!"

Tommy and Jessie ran off. Every kid, Tommy passed, high fived or waved at him. Jessie had a similar effect as he made more all-star teams, then anyone could count. Lee was still sitting there, he smiled at me. I was utterly dumbfounded.

"Hey, mind if I crash at your place tonight?" he said. Before I could utter a word, he jumped up. "Cool. Meet up at the courts after class."

With that, he walked away. I couldn't believe it. Just the day before, the only people that knew I existed beat the crap out of me. And now, three of the most popular kids in school sat down with me. I didn't know what had transpired, but maybe there was a God. And perhaps he didn't hate me after all. But if I didn't hurry off to class, I might be meeting him sooner than expected.

Chapter 2

What's in a Dry Loaf?

Lee walked home with me like he did yesterday, but this time he followed all the way to the door. I didn't know he was serious when he said he was planning on crashing at my place. I wasn't sure what to do.

He looked at me like, aren't you going to open the door?

I just stared, trying to figure out how to tell him I would need to call my mom and dad first and see if it was OK with them.

Then there was homework, and even though I knew I had an A in Bio, I still wanted to get 100 percent on my last test. Nobody at school had ever gotten an A on all of Mr. Heigan's tests and I had gotten a 100 percent on every test from the beginning of the year. It was like the one thing that I had made a goal that made school bearable. I knew even if I didn't study, I'd still probably ace it, but I couldn't risk it.

Then there was my journal. So much had happened today, and I really wanted to write for a while. Lee looked at me again and then looked embarrassed. Could he read my mind?

"Dude, so sorry," he said.

I didn't know what to say. Then Lee took his cigarette from his lips, licked his finger, extinguished the flame, and put it behind his ear. He looked at me like, OK, now we can go in.

At this point, I knew I would be total fodder if I said I had to call my parents first, so I did the brave thing, and let him in.

He walked in, the 1800-gallon saltwater tank that separated the living room from the dining room was the first thing he gravitated to. It really wasn't all that great compared to my parents' friend's, but I guess that didn't matter to him. He didn't say a word, he just stood there watching the fish. When the eel popped out its head, he smiled and said, "Dude." I walked by this every day and never really looked at it, but now it seemed magical.

"Want to see the game room?" I said.

"Dude."

I took it that this time, dude meant yes. I lead him out to the backyard, past the pool, to the pool house, which Dad converted into a game room a few years back. I marveled at how he found amazement in what I found to be mundane. The flashing arcade Packman, Centipede, and Gallica got his attention first.

His eyes wandered by the built-in bar next to the large screen T.V. and entertainment center. But those things didn't hold his attention. Instead, he immediately went for the pool table.

"Sorry," I said, "Dad's still refinishing it. It's like a hobby of his. He was telling me that it was a--"

"Medalist," Lee said, cutting me off, "1928, it used three pieces of the best slate instead of one, or wood, or shitty laminate for the playing surface." He rubbed his hand over the table and continued, "And its joints are secured by brass dowels and sockets, so it's entirely free from screw holes. One of the best tables ever made. Not like the crappy ones you find in pool halls."

"When it's finished, you'll have to come back over," I said.

"Dude."

"Do you like Atari?" I asked, and he nodded.

I went over to my gaming area. I had the games in order alphabetically, only because my favorite one was Adventure. Before that, I had organized them by genera and date. I so wanted to ask Lee to play Adventure, I had just found the secret room where Warren Robinett left his name. But I thought he might think I was a total dweeb if I offered that, then I thought how about chess? No, he would definitely believe I was totally lame then. I thought, how about a shooting game?

I blurted out, "How about Outlaw?" Completely forgetting he had just been released from Juvenile Hall. He looked at me like I was a jackass, and he was probably not too far off.

Without thinking, I vomited out another one of my favorite games, "Breakout?" but this was even less amusing to him.

I knew if I didn't save face soon, I was going to get an ass-kicking in my own home, "How about Pole Position?" Lee nodded. I handed him the controller, and he plopped down on the bean bag. I went over to the bar.

"Coke, Pepsi, or A&W?" I asked.

He didn't say anything, he just lifted his hand with a thumbs up. So, I brought over all three. He laughed when I got there, "Dude." He smiled politely and took the Pepsi.

We played for what seemed to be hours. The phone rang, and I let the machine pick it up. I knew it was Mom and Dad saying they weren't going to make it home, and this way, I wouldn't have to tell them Lee was over until tomorrow.

Typically, at this time of night, the house was dark, but at least it wasn't empty tonight. I brought out some pillows and sleeping bags and used the empty bag of chips to pick up the candy wrappers.

Lee looked around and took a sip of his Pepsi.

"Dude." He announced.

"What?"

"No, just dude."

"Everything OK?"

"You kidding? This is cool," he said.

"You're not bored?"

"You have no clue how good you got it."

I said, "Easy for you to say, you don't get your ass kicked every day."

"Not at school, but Vern kicks the crap out of me every chance he gets," Lee said.

"Your stepdad?"

Lee sighed, "Nah, he's just the flavor of the month.

"You know, my mom and dad are going to be gone for a few weeks this summer. If you want, you could stay here." I said.

"Where you going?" He asked.

"They're going to Europe, they go every year, medical lecturing, they don't take me. Mom's debating on what to do with me."

"Your mom and dad are doctors."

"Surgeons," I said. "Dad thinks I'll be OK alone, especially after my uncle abandoned me to go on a gambling bender last summer while they were gone." I looked at the empty bag of chips in front of Lee. "Want any more?"

"Good dude." He adjusted how he was sitting and looked totally uncomfortable. He reached into his pocket and pulled out his butterfly knife. "Damn thing always pokes me when I sit this way." He said as he put it back in a different pocket.

I asked, "Why did you tell everyone I beat up Jose L—"

"You did," he said, "Plus, I get caught fighting, it's back to juvie."

"What's that like?"

Lee looked curiously at me. The light of the video game flickered on his face. His tone changed and he said, "You're the first person to ask that."

"Really?" I asked.

Lee nodded, "Most people want to know what I did."

"I don't think you did anything."

"What?" He said in a stern voice.

"I mean, you're too cool. I just assumed you got a bad deal."

"So, you don't think I'm bad enough?"

"No, no, I don't," I said, "You're the nicest person I've ever met."

There was a long moment of silence. Lee looked down and said, "Juvie sucked."

"Sorry," I said.

"You really don't think I did anything?"

I nodded.

Lee looked at me in a new way, then nodded with respect and appreciation. And said, "Dude." But this dude felt very different from all the rest of the dudes he had used that day. He rolled over, and just like that, he was sound asleep. But I was totally unable to sleep.

I got up and headed back to the house to get my journal. I felt naked without it. I was like a journal junky. Hell, I'm still a journal junky. If I don't write in it, I can't sleep. Guess it's just my way of clearing all the crap from the day out of my head so I can rest.

On my way to my room, I stopped by the answering machine. I stared at it, and it stared back at me with its annoying red blinking eye. I pushed the play button.

"Hey Bud, sorry we missed you, hope you had a good day at school. We just got a call that there was a massive accident on the 5, so your mom and I will be in surgery all night. See you tomorrow."

Somehow this message seemed cold or was it me being bitter. There were many people my mom and dad would save that night, families that would be forever grateful they were there. But I didn't care, I wanted them here. Even with Lee sleeping across the way, it still felt like something was missing.

I went to my room and grabbed my journal. I was going to start writing, but I thought if Lee woke up and I wasn't there that that wouldn't be cool. I headed back. The light from the bar in the game room wasn't as good as the one on my desk, but I didn't want to be rude.

I sat there for a while, watching Lee sleep before I started writing. This was the first time someone my age came over and didn't make fun of me, and I had to make sure I didn't forget this night. My cousins, my mom and dad's friends with kids, and even neighbor's kids were mean to me. But not Lee, he was so good-hearted. There is no way he did anything wrong to end up in Juvenile Hall.

Maybe I should reconsider being a doctor and be a lawyer instead. That way, I can get Lee cleared and erase his record. I know I didn't write much tonight, but my eyelids are a bit too heavy to say much more, I'll just have to wait till tomorrow.

***

"Dude…Dude!" Lee said, pushing on me.

"What?" I said as I rubbed the crust out of my eyes.

"We got to go." He said in a whisper.

I looked at my Swatch and moved the pink guard band slightly, so I could see the hour hand better.

"It's like not even 5am yet." I plopped my head back down on my journal.

"Dude, come on." He insisted, "I need some duds."

"What?" I lifted my head and OH MY GOD, the crick in my neck, was awful.

"Some clothes," he said.

We left the game room. The deep blue sky reflected off the pool. The sun made its way up, turning it purple and then to pink in a matter of seconds. Mornings can be so cold, especially walking around the pool.

We got to my room, and Lee rummaged through my closet, tossing out clothes now and again. I would pick them up as soon as they hit the floor and refold them.

"Dude."

"What? " I said.

"You dress like a preppie... Oh, nice!" He found my beachwear section and grabbed one of my rip curl shirts. He again said nice when he got to my underwear drawer, he pulled out my Calvin Klein's and preceded to strip down and put them on.

It was a rather rude awakening. There he was in his birthday suit, with no issues, right in front of me. He had a tattoo of a butterfly mixed with skull and crossbones on his left hip. He caught me staring at it.

"What are you a fag or something!"

"No, just cool tattoo."

"Awe, OK." He finished pulling up the undies and must have sensed my uneasiness and said, "Don't worry, I'll wash them before I give them back." He smiled, slid on a pair of my 501 jeans, grabbed my Quicksilver jacket, and announced, "Let's go."

"I'm still in my pajamas."

"Dude!" This dude felt like it meant hurry the hell up and get with the program.

Chapter 3

Where do you go Sailing After Lunch?

You know when you get caught up in the moment or with conversation and completely forget all about where you are headed, or even where you are. Well, this was one of those moments. I followed Lee down a few streets utterly oblivious to my surroundings until I saw a few guys drinking out of paper bags.

I don't know why drunks think anyone would believe they were drinking anything but alcohol, like someone would take the time to cover up a Coke or orange juice with a paper bag so no one would know what they were drinking. But that's a rant for another time.

I had lost my bearings. Although it was in the general direction of the school, it seemed like we were on a detour of sorts. I didn't know what happened. I would typically never break a rule, never let anyone wear my clothes, or take me somewhere I didn't know. But there I was following Lee, without any clue of where we were headed. But for some strange reason, I was OK with it. Maybe deep down, I knew Lee would protect me if anything happened.

"Got any finals today?" He asked.

"Just Mr. Heigan's."

Lee laughed, "He's such a dick."

"I like him," I defended.

"You would."

The neighborhoods shifted from bad to worse. I became entirely in the dark about where we were and what we were doing. I had to ask.

"Umm... Where are we going?

"Cool, Vern's car's not there," Lee said.

He bolted up to this house that looked like the lawn had died twice and only grew back to die for a good Halloween effect. Lee went to the side door of the garage instead of the front door. "Come on!" he said as he pried the door open. "I need to get something."

I looked at my Swatch, "OK, but make it quick."

I couldn't help but think, that at any time, Jason or Michael Myers was going to peek around a corner with Freddy Krueger and kill me for entering this bad dream of a house.

We walked in, and I swear I saw a rat run across one of the supporting beams of the garage into a hole leading into the house. Lee wasn't the least bit affected by it, and I know he saw it too. He promptly went over to a stack of boxes, opened a lid, and dug through its contents.

"What are you looking for?" I asked.

"It's personal...just got to find it."

"If you tell me what it is, maybe I could help." He ignored me, opened another box, and dug through it frantically.

I looked at my watch. I mean, how well did I really know Lee? What if he was looking for drugs? Was I going to be in the middle of a drug bust? What would I tell my mom? And school! I had never been tardy in my whole life. I was in a panic and blurted out, "Hey, we gotta go!"

He opened yet another box and said, "Dude, go find a ladder or something... Wait! Do you hear that?"

I listened but didn't hear anything.

Lee looked petrified. "Dude!" with that and seeing the fear in his eyes, I nearly wet myself.

We scurried out of there and halfway down the block like two frightened mice. We soon slowed into a walk.

"Whatever you do, don't look back," Lee said.

Why the hell do people do that?! Why do they say things like that? All it does is force you into doing what they tell you not to do. It's like not laughing in church when someone farts. You can't suppress that kind of shit. Just like now, I had to look back.

An old copper Ranchero pulled into the driveway. The hood didn't match the rest of the car. It was a dull grey. The man that spilled out of it, who I assumed was Vern, looked like a haggard version of Mick Jagger. You could hear the bottles clanking on the ground as they fell out of the car with him. I don't remember ever hating anyone the first time I saw them until that moment. The utter disdain I had for a grown-up that could beat a kid. Especially one as cool as Lee. I was back to believing Lee was a good guy and felt terrible for thinking he could be involved with drugs.

***

We got to school ten minutes early which was ten minutes later than I like to. I stopped hyperventilating once I knew I could still get to class a little early.

"Hey, what period do you have, Mr. stick-up-his-ass?" Lee asked as we crossed the courtyard into the halls of the school.

"Mr. Heigan?" Lee nodded and laughed. I asked, "Why doesn't anyone like him?"

"Dude?"

"What?"

"OK, he's like the only teacher giving a final on the last day of school."

"But its finals week," I said, "isn't that what he's supposed to do?"

"Dude, finals week is for signing yearbooks and making plans for summer parties. Plus, that poser gives mad homework, and his tests are whack!"

"Why cause they're hard, and he expects us to work?" I asked.

"Dude. Damn straight!" he said.

"Isn't that what school is supposed to be?"

"Dude," Lee said in disagreement.

I shook my head and said, "Well, I got to go."

"Cool, I'll catch you after class," he said.

He walked off, disappearing into a crowd of kids. I didn't care what Lee thought this time. I liked Mr. Heigan. And hearing Lee call him names kind of pissed me off.

I got to the classroom but wasn't the first in line to get in, which added to my current frustrations. Today was not going the way I had planned it. Plus, I didn't review at all last night. I went to the back of the line to wait for the door to open.

That's when Sally Rhodes walked up and stood behind me with her friends Terra and Gina. Sally was by far the hottest girl in school. She wasn't stuck up and didn't need a cement truck to put on her cosmetics. No, not her, she had natural beauty. Long dark, gorgeous hair crystal blue eyes, and amazing in math. I never had the privilege of standing this close to her and had no clue she smelled as good as she looked. I mean, the vanilla scent of the Calvin Kline Obsession she was wearing had my head all tangled up in the clouds.

Then she spoke, and her voice on the ears was like warm honey on the tongue.

"This frigging blows," she said. "If I don't get at least like a 90 percent on this test I won't graduate."

"Sucks for you," Terra said, "Nobody gets an A on Heigan's tests."

"Not true," I blurted out.

I couldn't believe I just spoke to Sally and her friends. Was it that I was sleep-deprived and forgot my place? Maybe Lee needed to come over more often.

"Bullshit, Dover," Terra said, "bullshit nobody gets "A's" on his tests.

"I have, all year."

Gina laughed, "Ya, well, you don't count."

"I don't know about that," Sally said.

Didn't he kick Lòpez's ass?" asked Terra.

Sally smiled at me. She actually smiled at me. I damn near had an orgasm right then and there.

"Yeah, he did," Sally said.

I didn't even notice Mr. Heigan opening the door. I was momentarily tied up in a heavenly realm. As we all filtered in towards the entrance of the room, something radically changed in me. I didn't want my time with Sally to be over. I whispered to her, "Pick up two scantrons. Write your name on both and hand me one. I'll make sure you pass."

Sally asked, "Should I toss mine in the trash after?"

I panicked. "No. Take it home with you," I whispered.

I could just picture Mr. Heigan finding her test in the trash and expelling both of us.

She whispered to me, "Got it."

On the way in, I picked up a scantron, and she picked up two. We went to the back of the lab and sat cattycorner to each other. She was close enough that I could still smell her.

Sally quickly wrote her name on the first scantron and handed it to me. Her silky-smooth fingers grazed my hand.

Instantly I had an erection. And Oh My God, did it hurt. It was facing down and to the right before it expanded. And when it went fully erect, it got bent and tied up between the crease of my underwear and jeans. I almost screamed; I didn't care if anyone was looking, I had to move it back to center before I passed out.

After I fixed myself, I slid my scantron under hers. Now my heart was racing even faster. It dawned on me. I had just offered to cheat on a test. What the hell was I thinking?

Mr. Heigan announced, "OK, all books and bags away, please." He started passing out the tests.

I looked down, shit, I have the wrong one on top. I swapped the scantrons just before Heigan reached me.

"You'll have 40 minutes to finish." I looked at the clock, and it read 8:20. Mr. Heigan continued, "Please do not be tempted to cheat on your finals. Cause I will catch you. Keep in mind, people. I will throw out your worst test for the semester that includes this one. Just do your best, and good luck."

He was looking right at me. Did he see me swap out the tests? All I could think is that it was too late now, and I only had 40 minutes to complete two tests. I swapped out the scantrons putting Sally's on top again. And I rapidly went through the final, answering questions.

I looked up at the clock when I was close to finishing her test. It read 8:45. Crap I was behind.

Mr. Heigan got up from his desk and did his regular halftime walk behind each kid in the class. I penciled in the last two bubbles on Sally's test and quickly put mine over hers and started back at the beginning of the test. I knew I had to fly cause if I wasn't at least halfway through by the time he got to me, then he would know something was up.

The clock read 8:50, and Mr. Heigan just walked up to the second to the last row right before mine. I got to move faster, I said to myself. Then it dawned on me. If we both got a hundred percent, he would know we cheated. Crap, how do I do this? I went through my head and figured with his grading scale that I had to miss at least seven questions to get an 85%. But wait, I had never got less than an A on anything. Ever. In my whole life. What the hell was I doing?!

I looked up, and the clock read 8:55. Mr. Heigan stopped behind me watching. He never stayed that long behind me before. I felt the beads of sweat forming on my face, I looked at the scantron, and my heart sunk. The one under it was slightly visible. I only had one question left to answer when Mr. Heigan put his finger on the test next to where the bottom scantron was showing through.

"What's this?" He said.

I froze.

"Dover," he said, disappointed, "we both know you're better than this."

I glanced at Sally. She looked terrified, which didn't do anything to help dislodge my heart from my throat. I calmly answered the last question, I had meant to get it wrong, but since I was busted anyway, I figured I just bubble my last bubble with the right answer.

Mr. Heigan whispered, "Nice. See, I know you could do it." He patted me on the back and walked back to his desk.

Sally and I let out a massive sigh of relief. With that, a buzzer on Mr. Heigan's desk rang.

OK, everyone," Mr. Heigan announced, "pass your scantrons forward. Also, have a great summer.

Sally stashed her scantron in her bag. And when the kid next to me passed me his test, I put it between Sally's and mine, so they weren't next to each other and handed them to the kid next to me.

The school bell rang, and we all hurried out of class.

I was in such shell shock from the experience I didn't even notice Sally following so close behind me.

"So?" she said to me.

"What?"

"How do you think I did?"

"Oh, no worries, you got an A."

She screamed, hugging me as if we were long lost lovers. At least that's the way I like to remember it. But every detail of this part is totally accurate. She kissed me. Sally Rhodes kissed me. So what if it was on the cheek. It was awesome. I've never forgotten any detail of that first kiss. It was so soft, with the sweet scent of Obsession, and then her breath on my neck still gives me goosebumps to this day.

The best moments in life just don't last anywhere near long enough. I stayed in the mystical daze she put me in as long as I could. Even watching her walk away was magical. Then it hit me. I could have been the first student in the history of the school to have aced every single Heigan test. It was my dream at the start of the day, but I knew he would have known she was cheating if we had both aced it, so I settled for a B. Looking back, I know it was wrong and idiotic. Still, in all honesty, it was totally worth it.

"Dude," Lee said, pulling me out of my moment.

"What?" I said.

"Come on."

I followed him out through the school gates. Just before I could tell him that we were breaking the rules, Jessie pulled up in the coolest V.W. bus I had ever seen. An absolutely stunning and rare 1967 Volkswagen Safari Window bus. The genuine 13-window Deluxe V.W., which in my opinion may just be one of the nicest V.W. buses on the planet. The exterior was a two-tone Titan red and cream with the iconic split front windshield, roof rack, and six pop-out side windows. All the exterior chrome looked brand new. A timeless piece of moving art.

Tommy stuck his head out the passenger window and said, "Hey! You dick-wads want a ride?"

Lee jokingly quipped back, "Blow me."

Sorry, no magnifying glass dude. Tommy quipped as Jessie laughed. Lee proceeded to open the side door and hopped in. He looked at me.

"Dude." He said, and I am sure this dude meant, come on, let's go.

"School's not out yet," I said.

"Live a little." He said

"Come on, we always ditch the last day of school," Tommy added.

"Come on, Dude, no way to get busted. Now hop in."

Chapter 4

The end or The Beginning?

You guessed it, I hopped in the bus. I thought, well, I cheated, and it got me the most amazing kiss of all time. Who knew, maybe we'd run into Sally while we were out caravanning around, or perhaps some other magnificent thing could happen.

We ended up at Tommy's place. He used the garage as a place to hang, as he called it. This crowded space had all manner of surf posters covering the walls, some carpet remnants on the floor, and a broken-beat-up couch was its centerpiece.

I was playing basketball with Lee. More or less, I was retrieving the ball every time he made a shot and seldom put one in myself. Tommy and Jessie were making me crazy going back and forth, trying to solve a Rubik's Cube. I wanted to grab it out of their hands and solve it, but they had a running bet on who could do that first. And I knew I had to leave it alone until they invited me to help solve it.

A car pulled in front of Tommy's house. Tommy's mom and dad got out of the car, yelling at each other.

"It's your fault!" she yelled.

"How is it my fault?" his dad quipped back.

"You're too soft!"

"I'm too soft? I'm too soft!? Whatever." Tommy's dad stormed into the house. He was followed closely by Tommy's mom.

She yelled, "Don't you, whatever me! What about my feelings, what about what I need!"

Tommy's mom slammed the front door behind her.

There was this uncomfortable silence. Jessie, Lee, and Tommy silently put away stuff. I joined in. Tommy apologetically looked at us and said, "I'm sorry you had to see this." I think I just automatically started to know what he meant when he simply said *dude*, or at least I thought I knew.

The yelling coming from inside the house intensified. It was when we could clearly hear things being broken inside that we piled into Jessie's V.W. bus and sped off.

I watched Tommy fiddle with the Rubik's Cube in the rear-view mirror. He looked back at my reflection and said, "Five bucks buys you in."

I wanted to correct him and say, dollars, bucks are animals, but I knew for sure that wouldn't go over well, so I just said, "OK."

Lee added, "That will bring the pot up to 20."

"Cool," I said, "I could use an extra 20."

They all laughed at me until after a few calculated turns, I solved it.

"Dude look," Lee said.

"No way!" Tommy retorted.

Jessie just laughed, "You two should have known better. Come on, he's like a mad genius." Without missing a beat, he changed the subject. "Hey, I need to stop by the house real quick."

Something didn’t add up. I played baseball with Jessie, and the teams only had a two-year age gap per division. There was no way he could be sixteen. I had to know.

"I thought you were only a year older than me," I said to Jessie.

"Nope. Two years. I'll be fifteen next week."

"How did you get a driver's license then?"

Lee and Tommy erupted in laughter in the back of the bus. Jessie smiled and looked at me like I was from another planet. And maybe I was. I mean, I wouldn't have even gone to the same school if they hadn't redrawn the district lines that year. And let's face it, I lived in the hills, and they lived in the valley. But when I got to thinking about it, I was having more fun than I had ever had, so maybe being in the hills wasn't all it was cracked up to be.

It was kind of cool Jessie didn't care about having a driver's license. Jessie parked in front of the house and said, "Wait here." He seemed overly concerned about something. He hopped out of the car, and I looked at Lee and Tommy like what's going on.

"His dad's got cancer, bad," Lee said.

"To the max. That's why he drives." Tommy followed.

"What about his mom?" I asked.

"She bailed a long time ago," Lee added.

"Totally, and he’s like all his dad’s got for help," Tommy said.

"I need some smokes, hey go see how much longer," Lee said.

"I thought he said to wait?" I asked.

"Don't be a wuss." Lee and Tommy said in unison.

I got the distinct feeling like I was meant to be their lackey. None the less, I got out of the car, walked up to the house, and knocked on the door. Jessie answered and put up a finger to say, "hold on." I wanted to go in and help, but he seemed adamant that I stay at the door. I watched him help his dad from a wheelchair to a bed in the living room.

On the wall above the bed were several MVP awards with Jessie's name on them, next to models of F-14 fighter jets. Jessie kissed his dad on the forehead and walked out. He met up with me at the door and said, "Come on, let's go."

I remembered having his dad as a coach and how strong he was. Seeing him like this made me want to be a doctor again, so I could come up with a cure and heal him. We pulled out of the driveway, and I couldn't get the image of this frail old man that used to be in better shape than my dad, being helped up from a wheelchair.

"Crap," Jessie said.

"What?" I said.

"I need gas, come on divvy up!"

"Come on, I need smokes," Lee said.

"Your needle says you have a full tank?" I added.

Jessie pointed to a pad of paper with a bunch of numbers on it. I quickly got it. The needle on the gas gauge was stuck, so Jessie kept a log of when to fill up.

“I'm broke.” Lee said, “Besides Tommy's into me for a grip, he can pay.”

Tommy said, "Come on, I can't right now." to Jessie.

"Not cool! You know it's your guy's turn for gas."

"I'll pay for it," I said.

"Nice, bro." Lee and Tommy said in unison.

We pulled into a gas station on the self-service side. I got out with Jessie to pay and help pump the gas. I noticed a bumper sticker on the left bumper of the bus, it had a blue fighter jet that read: "Air Force, Experience a great way of life." Lee bolted inside and, in just a few short moments, came out with a red-topped cigarette box. He pulled out his zippo, and Jessie eyed him.

"Don't even think about it," Jessie said.

"Come on!" Lee yelled.

"I mean it, not in my bus!" Jessie yelled back.

"Seriously?!" Lee asked.

"Serious as a heart attack," Jessie answered, "No cancer sticks in my bus!"

"Then hurry up!" Lee said. I was glad he told him he couldn't smoke. I didn't care much for them. Although if anyone could make smoking look cool, Lee could. But to be honest, I hated he did it mostly because I liked him.

Lee put the cigarette away. Jessie looked at me and said, "I'm losing my dad to those damn things, I won't have that shit lit in my bus." After he said that, I was entirely on board with him.

We all piled back into the bus, and off we went. We hadn't passed more than one light before having to stop for a red one. Lee yelled, "Drill it!" They flung open the doors to the bus. Jessie, Lee, and Tommy hopped out and ran around it. They all jumped back in, just before the light changed. It was so scary at first, but when we sped off, and nothing terrible happened, I decided I would jump out the next time they yelled drill it.

It was getting dark, and we ended up at the scary place Lee and I were in that morning, but it was even scarier at night.

Lee hopped out and said, "I'll be right back. Keep it running."

No one said anything. We sat there in silence. It was clear to me that we were the getaway car. We watched Lee disappear into the house. He was only in there a few seconds before he came flying back out, followed closely by Vern, the haggard-looking guy I saw that morning.

Vern stopped just outside the door and yelled at Lee, "You're both friggin' proof that evolution can go sideways. Do you hear me, you piece of shit! I said, where's your mom! You know you're a user, a worthless user, just like your mom. Get back here, you lazy maggot. I'm talking to you! Hey! This isn't over yet."

Lee made a b-line to us, ignoring Vern. He hopped into the bus, and we drove off. I knew the odds were that my mom and dad would definitely be home tonight, they never got more than three shifts in a row, and I wasn't sure how to tell them about Lee. But I didn't want him to have to go back to Vern's house either. I made up my mind that I would invite Lee over and worry about my mom and dad later.

"Where too?" Jessie said.

Before I could see if Lee wanted to stay with me, Tommy looked at him and asked, "Want to crash with me at my cousin's?" Lee nodded, and Tommy asked Jessie, "Do you remember how to get to Takumi's?"

"Off Beach and Warner in Fountain Valley, right?"

"Dude, you rock."

"I know," he turned to me and said, "I'll drop you off first. I was relieved and bummed all at the same time. Part of me was glad that I wouldn't have to have an awkward moment with my parents, but there was another side. One that felt jealousy. I wanted to be the one Lee felt safe with. Also, I really liked having him over. It was weird feeling mad at Tommy for just being kind to Lee.

We drove up to my place. I had them drop me off just before the driveway, I waved, and they were gone. Wow, what a day. As I walked up the driveway, I saw the 911 was out, which meant there was a Porsche club event soon. I hated those club events. They gave a whole new meaning to dullness.

All the lights were on. It was a good bet Mom and Dad were both home and waiting for me. At this point, I knew I was going to have some explaining to do.

I walked in, and Dad said, "Hey, hurry up, we have dinner reservations!"

"Make sure you put on a clean shirt and tie," Mom added.

I rushed off to my room, surprised that there was no Spanish Inquisition about where I had been all afternoon. Or were they saving it for dinner?

***

I sat there in the restaurant, debating about what to tell them. They didn't seem to have a clue about what had transpired over the last few days, but I'm a horrible liar, so I told them everything. Well, almost everything. I kind of left out the ditching, Sally, and that Lee went to Juvie.

OK, so I didn't tell them everything, which was actually a first for me. No, really, I always was honest. Well, except last summer, but that's different. Uncle John made me promise, plus he said what they didn't know wouldn't hurt them. He definitely didn't want them to know he put my math skills to practical use at the tables. Of course, that was when Vegas really didn't pay much attention to whether kids were in a bar or not.

I did tell them about how Lee saved me from José, and how he'd been walking me home, and him spending the night and hanging out with Tommy and Jessy, and about how evil Vern was. They listened intently to every word. Then they exchanged glances and smiled at me.

Dad said, "That's great."

I looked shocked. I thought to myself, was this a Twilight Zone episode, or were these really my parents? Mom followed with, "We're glad you're finally making friends, honey." This, by the way, didn't make me feel at all better. I felt even more socially inept than I had before. I was glad not to be in trouble, but it kind of sucked knowing my parents were worried about my social inadequacies.

"Yes, and if this Lee character needs a place to stay, he's always welcome,"

Dad said, turning to my mom, "Remember Ray?" She nodded, "His dad was a real piece of work too. He was drunk all the time. Ray spent most of his time at our place, even went to college with me."

"So… You're not mad at me?" I asked or more like stated.

"No, but just page me the next time," and Mom said, "As long as you make sure to always clean up after yourselves, I have no issue with it."

"Yeah, Bud, you've never given us any reason not to trust you. You're getting older, and we understand these things."

"OK, cool," I said, "Would it be OK if they could come over on Saturday and hang out?"

“Of course, but are you sure you want to miss the Porsche show this weekend?” Mom asked.

“I'm good with that,” I said.

To my surprise, both my mom and dad were excited that I was having friends come over. On the one hand, it was great. I wasn't in trouble. But on the other hand, I didn't particularly like how my mom and dad viewed me. The upside was I didn't have to go hang out with my parents and stuffy old people. Instead, I would get to stay at home and play games all day with my friends. Life was looking so much easier.

***

Unfortunately, no one showed up that Saturday. I didn't know Jessie's phone number, and by the time I walked to his house, he was gone. And Vern scared the hell out of me, so there was no way I was going to walk down there alone. As far as alone goes, I felt even lonelier than I had before. It was a worse feeling than I had ever had. I can't find words to describe it. Maybe I was depressed, but who knows, right? I mean, how do we describe something that's inside us that can’t be seen? And how do we really even know if it's the same thing as what someone else describes, right? I just knew I hurt real bad inside.

About two weeks went by before Lee showed back up at my doorstep. It was a good thing because I had spent too much time contemplating why breathing was all that important. I have to say seeing him again made me feel instantly better. I think being isolated from your peers is a bad thing.

Dad finally finished the pool table, and I couldn’t wait to show Lee. I don’t know what it was about that table, but as soon as Lee played on it once, he was addicted to it. Lee started coming over all the time. The weird thing was he seemed to have parent radar. Never once did he show up when my mom and dad were home. They still hadn’t met him and they were only a day away from leaving. On this particular day, Lee had convinced the others to hang out at my place too.

Tommy, Lee, and I were playing a game of pool. Tommy looked around at the arcade games, the bar and then out the window at the Olympic sized pool where Jessie was walking by and said,

"Why didn't we hang here?"

Jessie walked in visibly, upset, and I asked him if he was OK. He responded, "Aunt May just took dad to San Diego!”

"Does that mean you're gone too?" Lee asked.

"Not yet, she's leaving me to clean out the house, box anything I want. Then uncle' dick wad' will be coming to stay and get the place ready to sell!" Jessie said. He was holding back so much emotion. His hands shook, and his eyes were welled with tears. But even though you could see clearly he was ready to cry, no tears fell down his cheeks.

"That's bogus. Bogus crap is raining down on all of us." Tommy added.

I asked, "What?"

Jessie motioned to Tommy, "His parents dropped the big D."

"Like we didn't see that coming a mile away," said Lee.

I said, "That sucks. If I got a D, I would be so dead."

Tommy looked at me like I was nuts and said, "What?"

"Divorce – they're cutting out on him," Lee said to me.

"Oh," I said. Something about the way he said that hit me. He didn't use the word parents, mom, or dad, he used the word they. And the delivery of it was so cold. It was strange, I got the feeling he didn't trust adults at all. But then again, could you blame him? His mom was never around, we all knew she did drugs, and Vern was, well, Vern.

Jessie went on, saying, "That bites."

"No shit," Tommy said, "My dad's taking a job in Chicago. I can't hang without a beach. I'll lose it, I swear!"

"Harsh," said Jessie.

I couldn't imagine what Tommy was going through. Then again, I don't remember my parents ever talking to each other the way Tommy's parents did. I'd only been over to his place once, but they really did go at each other. There was something else I noticed even more than the arguing because even my mom and dad did that sometimes.

When they did argue, my mom would still give my dad a smile from across the room, or there would be a compliment my dad would give on shoes my mom must have worn a hundred times. Or even the way they folded laundry together during an argument seemed loving in some strange, messed up way.

"We have to do something crazy this summer, make it bad," Lee said. I thought to myself, why would anyone in their right mind want things to be worse than they were? I couldn't let this nagging thought go, so I did what I always did and, by the way, still do, and asked, "Why?"

"Why what?" Lee asked.

"Why bad?" I asked.

"Bad is good," Jessie explained. “It’s like when something is better than good, like a tricked-out car or a totally fantastic time you say it’s ‘bad,’ got it?”

“Why don’t you just say we had a totally cool time?” I asked.

"I got it! Endless summer!" Tommy announced.

"You’re joking, right?" Lee asked.

"We don't know how to surf." Jessie quipped.

Lee tacked on, "And boards are hell-a expensive."

"What's an endless summer?" I asked.

Tommy quickly answered, "It's what we're going to have! Think about it. Jessie's bus, beaches, and Bettys."

Lee nodded, "Pretty bad, but still need green."

Jessie looked at Lee and said, "Just sell your mom's stash."

"Hey! Not cool." Lee retorted.

"Like she'd have any leftovers," Tommy said, laughing.

Lee tackled Tommy, pinning Tommy to the ground. Lee licked his finger and kept sticking it in Tommy's ear. As they rolled around on the floor, I thought about my stash of cash. I hadn’t spent any of my birthday money in a long time. Never really needed to. I probably had a few hundred dollars, and then there was the sealed envelope Uncle John gave me last summer for helping him out. He said to leave it sealed until I got to college, but I’m sure my mom and dad had that covered.

"OK, already, get off, you dick!" Tommy yelled at Lee.

"I have some money." I blurted out.

"DAH! Like we couldn't tell." Jessie said.

Followed by Tommy, "You’re brilliant! You could like, use your peep's plastic."

"Totally!" Lee said in agreement as he pulled balls from the pockets and placed them in the triangular rack.

Jessie nodded, saying, "That would be so bad!"

"We could be gone weeks!" Tommy said.

I pretended that I didn't hear what I thought I had heard and said, "I only have a couple hundred dollars. I—"

Tommy cut me off, saying, "No, dude, just lift a card from your parents."

I think I was still in shock, how was this ok with everyone. I started to feel like I missed something, like I was an alien from another planet. I stated what I thought would have been evident to them all, "But it's not mine." I said.

"Yeah, like, by the time they get the bill, we'll be back, and they'll report it stolen. No harm in that." Lee stated.

"But that's lying," I said.

"Technically, it's stealing," said Lee.

"I can't," I said. There was no way I would steal from my own parents. What was wrong with everyone?

"Dude, come on," Tommy begged.

Followed by Jessie's "Man up, dude."

"No!" I said, "It's not right."

Jessie and Tommy gave me pressuring looks. All of a sudden, what started as a great day turned awful.

Tommy continued with, "Don't be such a buzzkill!"

Followed by Jessie, saying, "I knew he was a poser!"

I was just about to throw them all out and tell them to leave. But Lee looked at me. He saw how upset I was and changed. His furrowed brow softened, Lee nodded at me and smiled. He knew my world had a different set of rules. He glared at the others; they instantly knew that he wanted them to stop. It was like watching the alpha dog in a pack take control.

"Leave him alone," Lee announced.

"But--" Tommy said.

"Give it a rest!" Lee said.

"Fine." said both Jessie and Tommy. They gave me one last look of disappointment and left. As they did so, Lee walked over to me, he patted me on the shoulder, picked up his pool cue, chalked it, and eyed the table. His eyes glanced over the racked balls at the end of the table as he placed the scarred cue ball just in the right place.

"When are you going to learn how to live a little?" He said as he pulled back the pool cue and slammed it into the cue ball. The sound of the cue ball crashing into the others was louder now that the room had been silenced. A rainbow of colors spun around the table. It was like watching the fish in the saltwater tank at feeding time.

I'll never forget how Lee managed to sink the striped yellow and solid yellow ball on the break. It was almost magical, like some of the card tricks I had worked on. I knew he had sent the others off, but I had to make it clear to him.

"I can't steal from my parents!" I said.

"Don't they usually give you anything you ask for?" he said as he sank another ball. I didn't really expect that as a comeback. It didn't seem to address what I had just said at all.

"Not everything," I said.

He looked around the room. "Seriously?" he hit the cream-colored cue ball so precisely that it circled around the black of the eight-ball without touching it. It connected with a red striped ball knocking it smoothly into the corner pocket. I found myself mesmerized by his talent for the game.

I wanted to make sure he understood my position, as he seemed to be avoiding a direct understanding of my situation. I said, "I can't! My parents would never trust me again. My life would be over as I know it!"

Lee sunk the last striped ball and asked, "Thought you said they left you with a gambling addict last summer?"

"Uncle John? Well, he's always had his issues. Not their fault—"

"So, they knew he had issues, and left you with him anyway," Lee knocked in another ball.

"It's not like that," I said.

"Hey, defend them all you want. But the truth is, you only get one life." Lee pointed out his shot, took it, and sank the eight ball. "And the only person you can ever trust is yourself."

I looked at the table, and he had put every striped ball in without a scratch or a miss. And the only solid missing was yellow.

Chapter 5

What's life without a Holiday in Reality?

Mom and Dad rolled out their luggage into the living room. Dad set his leather Ralph Lauren bags next to Mom's Gucci suede travel purse. Mom had bathed in Obsession, Dad's favorite perfume, which was the only difference between the two of them. They both wore pink polo shirts, tan slacks, and Gucci loafers; their standard airplane attire.

"Did you get everything?" Dad asked.

Mom went through an invisible checklist that looked like it was right in front of her. Dad went to talk again, but she held up her hand, shushing him, and replied, "I'll double-check the office. Why don't you double-check our room?"

He nodded, and they left the room.

And there it was. Dad's fanny pack sitting there on top of the luggage. I looked around. I knew I had at least a good five minutes before they came back.

I got up slowly and walked over to their luggage. With each step, my heart pounded harder. There it was, now right in front of me. The tarnished leather fanny pack sat there, just daring me to open it. As my hand moved to it, my heart jumped to my throat. I unzipped it, Dad's wallet protruded out, and I picked it up.

I saw Mom rounding the corner back into the living room. I quickly stuffed it back into the pack.

"Shit!" She said, "Oh, sorry, honey. I didn't see you there. I'll be right back." And she hurried off.

The coast was clear again. I pulled the wallet back out and opened it. In the back of it was a platinum Visa that looked brand new. I pulled it out, put it in my pocket, and quickly stuffed Dad's wallet back into the fanny pack. I could hear my dad's footsteps and knew he was close. The zipper jammed. I tried to force it, but it slid out of my hands, falling to the floor. I watched in horror as all the contents spilled out. I frantically dropped to my knees, shoving everything back into it.

"Hey, sport." My dad said, then he paused and said, "What are you doing?" My heart was pounding, and I couldn't even come up with a bad excuse.

"Hey, honey," Mom interrupted, "Did you get the conference notes? I couldn't find them."

"No!" Dad exclaimed, "It's in the den. Be right back." I stood up and slowly slid the fanny pack back onto the luggage. I didn't know what had just happened, but I was in a panicked daze.

"Thank you, dear," she said to me, "Sure, you don't want to go to your uncle's? Three weeks is a long time alone, honey."

Dad walked back in, "Got it!" He looked at my mom and said, "And it's two weeks and a couple days in transit, quit exaggerating."

"Maybe we should have my brother come down again."

"I'll be fine," I said.

"We only had to bail him out of jail once." Dad quipped.

"That's not fair!"

"I'll be fine, really," I said.

"You're right, I'm still out that bond money." Dad continued.

Mom shot him a disapproving glare, "It seems too long."

"He'll be fine, right Bud?" I nodded, and Dad continued, "Plus, Maria will be here every other day taking care of the place, and she has our numbers."

With that, Mom walked me to the telephone and showed me a list she taped on the wall next to the phone.

"Now, I have color-coded all the numbers. Pink is emergencies, yellow is—"

"He will be fine. Come on, we got to go already. If we miss this flight, we are S.O.L." Dad walked over to help escort Mom out and rubbed my head. "Be good," he said.

"See you soon, honey." Her gold crucifix necklace dangled in front of my face as she bent down and kissed me on the head... My mom's an Irish Catholic, and my dad's a practicing Baptist. They had great theological debates and enjoyed it.

The doorbell rang, and a shuttle driver came in and grabbed their bags. My dad put on his fanny pack. And Mom grabbed her purse.

The door closed.

I walked back to the table and sat down. I heard the shuttle pull away, and soon its motor was inaudible. I pulled out my dad's credit card and put it on the table.

I've gone to both Sunday schools, and I'm pretty sure the guilt I was feeling was instilled by the Catholic one. I spun the card on the table like a coin. In the card spinning, I actually could see the image of Lee popping José Lòpez in the nose. It still wasn't too late to put the card in their room, but I kept seeing José's fist smashing into my face. Lee risked going to jail instead of turning the other cheek for my benefit.

Lee just lived life, why couldn't I? I think that is why they left Jesus' childhood out of the Bible, cause being a kid sucked.

I watched the sun come up and still didn't know what I wanted to do. There was a knock on the front door. Did my mom and dad come back? Did they find out I took the card already? Then I was mad at myself for being so stupid, they had a key why would they knock? Plus, the door was unlocked. It wasn't the pool guy. He had a gate key and only came on Fridays. It was only nine in the morning, and deliveries never came before noon. Then the doorbell rang. What was my issue? Why didn't I just answer the stupid door instead of trying to guess who was there?

I got up and walked over to the door, still trying guess at who was there, and when I opened it, Lee stood there in front of me with a new bruise on his face. "Before you say anything, I need to say I'm sorry about me and the guys yesterday. I put them in their place." He apologized. I could tell he was sincere. "So, we're all good, right?" he asked. I felt relieved.

He gave me a big hug. And I invited him in.

"Hey, so we were talking. Is it cool if we like through a bad pool party here tonight?" My gut instantly knotted up. I don't know what sounded worse, having a bunch of kids over destroying my home, or using my dad's credit card to fund a surf trip. I knew if I kept saying no all the time, it wouldn't be long before I was by myself again.

"I like the idea of an endless summer." I announced. Lee looked at me with a halfcocked smile and said, "You didn't."

I pulled out my dad's credit card.

"No way!" Lee said. He gave me an even bigger hug and said, "let's get everyone over here!"

***

The plan was to be gone for a max of two weeks, camp out at all the beaches from Huntington to San Diego. We raided my house for food, soda, and camping gear. I stuffed the most essential thing in my backpack, which, of course, was my journal. I never went anywhere without that.

I packed a duffle bag with the other essentials. Like ten pairs of underwear, one can never have too many of those, a toothbrush, toothpaste, sunscreen, lots of sunscreen, and most of the stuff hanging in the beachwear section of my closet.

I pulled out the bottom file drawer of my desk. Behind it taped to the back was Uncle John's sealed envelope. I peeled off the tape, pulled it off, and put the drawer back in. Of course, those stupid draws never go back in as easy as they pull out, and it was taking me forever. Lee popped his head in and said, "Let me get that," He grabbed my duffle bag. I wanted to open up the envelope, but not in front of Lee or the others. He stood there staring at me.

"Give me a minute," I said. Lee stood there and waited patiently. I stuffed the envelope in my backpack and figured I'd look at it later when I had a minute alone.

We hopped on the bus and headed out to Jack's Surf Shop in Huntington Beach. I sat in the back of the bus. Prince's song, "Let's Go Crazy" came on the radio. Jessie and Tommy started singing along. Lee joined in.

On the one hand, this was the happiest I had ever been, but yet at the same time, it was the worst I had ever felt. I was betraying my mom and dad. But why not enjoy a vacation?

Last summer, after Mom and Dad got back from Europe; we spent a week together in New Zealand in a Presidential Suite. Tommy, Jessie, and Lee might never get to experience anything like that. I wasn't going to report the card stolen.

I couldn't go that far. I'd just tell my parents to take it out of my college fund or to not take me on their next few trips, or something. The more I thought about my parents, the more I wondered if it wasn't too late to change my mind. I mean we hadn't got to a store yet, and I used my own money to put gas in the bus. Plus I had Uncle John's envelope.

"You deal," Lee plopped a deck of cards right in front of me.

"Don't bet him anything," Tommy said, laughing, "Nobody ever beats him at cards."

"Don't listen to him, he's just bitter cause he's into me for a carton after last night," Lee said.

"He probably doesn't even know how to play," Tommy said to Lee. Jessie laughed.

"I know a little about cards," I said. This was one of those times when I knew I could shine. I had never had the upper hand on any of them. Lee was way better at playing pool, Tommy could totally kick my ass on any of my video games, and I didn't stand a snowball's chance in hell at beating Jessie at hoops. But cards, poker was my game. I asked, "Poker?"

Lee nodded, "Want to raise the stakes?"

"Sure, I'm game," I said. I couldn't wait to show off my skills.

"Ok, I win; you owe me cigarettes," Lee said.

"And if I win?" I asked.

"Not gonna happen, so it doesn't matter," Lee said. Tommy and Jessie looked at each other and laughed.

I shook my head and said, "There has to be some kind of stakes, or it's no fun."

"Sure, if it makes you happy, you can have whatever you want."

"Anything I want?"

"Sure," Lee said as he laughed.

"OK," I said.

I remembered how my uncle said anyone can stack a deck and deal from the bottom if they're fast enough. But a real artist can not only shuffle the cards so that they are precisely where you want them, but they also know exactly where their opponent will cut the deck. There's also one other step in magic tricks we use to do this as well, but I promised my uncle I would never reveal it, and a promise is a promise.

After feeling the weight of the cards in my hand and a few shuffles, I felt confident. I handed Lee the deck, and he cut it exactly where I needed him to. I dealt him three aces but gave myself a royal flush, that is, if Lee discarded two of his five cards to go after the Ace of Spades that I was holding in my hand.

"You want to up the bet?" he said, "How about two boxes of cigarettes?"

"Ok," I said, but if I win, you have to go two whole days without smoking."

Lee smiled and put down two cards, "You're on." He looked at Tommy and said, "It's like stealing candy from a baby."

I dealt him two more cards and set down two of mine and picked up two more from the deck. I was relieved to see I hadn't messed up. I looked concerned just to mess with Lee. He put down his aces and said, "Read'em and weep."

"I'm not sure, but I think this might beat yours," I set down my royal flush.

Lee's jaw dropped, "OK! Best two out of three."

"OK," I said. Jessie tilted the rear-view mirror so he could watch along with Tommy. I went on to win the next game.

"Let's go again," I said, "I'll have you smoke-free in no time." Lee flipped me off. Tommy and Jessie's laughter was contagious, so I laughed along with them.

Lee glared at me, "Ha, ha, don't be a dick!"

I smiled and shuffled the deck. I wanted to try one of my tricks with actual people instead of my saltwater friends. I fanned the cards in front of Lee and said, "pick one." Lee did somewhat reluctantly. I put the deck back together and said, "Slide it into the middle of the deck." He slid the Ace of Spades back into it, then I said, "Take the top card off the deck." He did, "Is that your card?"

"No."

"Humm, Tommy, can you see the card in his hand?" Tommy nodded, "Ok, don't forget what it is."

"OK."

I chucked the cards against the widow. Only one stuck to the window. It was the Jack of Clubs; it was the one that had been in Lee's hand.

Tommy's eyes went wide, "Dude!"

I said to Lee, "Now is the card in your hand the right one?"

Lee looked down at his hand, "Dude! No way!" He revealed his card, and it was the Ace of Spades.

With that, Jessie pulled into a metered space right in front of Jack's. My heart sunk, was I actually going to do this? They all piled out of the car, and I just followed.

Tommy walked in, and the place came alive when he hollered, "WhaZ Up!" The sales guys came up and gave him a hug. "These are my bros, can you hook 'em up with some sweet boards?"

"Dude, Cha." The sales guy said.

"Hey, Tommy," said this old surfing guy.

Tommy smiled, "Sup, Mikey."

"Not the waves," he said, "pretty blown out today."

“Not a prob today, bro. Got a bunch of barneys, they just need to be good enough to get up.”

There was definitely a whole new language I was going to have to learn so I could understand what was going on around me. I studied Spanish and Latin and was about to take Greek with a private tutor. Latin was pretty hard in the beginning. What these guys spoke was not only hard to understand but seemed nonsensical. I was bound and determined to figure it out, though.

The old surfer Mikey said, “They got boards?”

“Na, but my cuz here will hook ‘em up.”

“If you’re in the market, I got a Retro Twin Fin by Mark Richards.”

“No way!”

“Way.”

Tommy looked at me with wanting eyes.

I gathered that meant he wanted it real bad.

“I’ll trade in Sammy, OK?”

“OK?” I didn’t know what the hell a Sammy was, but it seemed to have some kind of value. Tommy darted out, and Jessie and Lee looked at me like I was the coolest guy in the room. I had no idea why, though. Tommy came rushing back in with his board, which I figured had to be Sammy, and we were ushered to the backroom of surfboards.

The surfboards all looked pretty much the same to me, but I was assured they were all very different. Tommy looked like I did the day I got my Atari for Christmas. He held his new board like it was his new best friend.

Tommy and Cuz talked about all kinds of stuff that made no sense to me at all. Still, when it was all said and done they said we would have the most fun on the Malibu surfboards, also known as funboards, it was kind of a blend between a longboard and a shortboard. Why they just didn't say that to start with is beyond me. We picked out new boards, more or less the colors, Tommy picked out the type and size of each of the surfboards. Then we all got what they call spring suits, which were wet suits with the legs cut off them, some hats, and sunglasses.

He had his “Cuz” ring us up. They didn’t look related at all, Tommy was Asian, and his Cuz was whiter than me, if that was at all possible. The only thing they seemed to have in common was bad bleach jobs.

It was all fun and games until Cuz totaled out all the stuff we had gotten. It actually took my breath away. I had expected it to cost a lot, but this was way more than I had even imagined. This was it. There was no turning back now. I felt as sick as I did when I had the flu a few months back. I reached into my pocket and grabbed the piece of plastic with my dad's name on it and set it on the counter.

“Dude, platinum.” Cuz proclaimed to the entire store. He pulled out a carbon receipt and put it in the card on the imprinter and the carbon-receipt on top of it. I watched him slide the impression wheel back and forth over it. There it was my dad’s name staring at me boldly. Cuz pulled out the receipt, ripped off a yellow section of it, and handed it to me. At that moment, I’m sure I looked as yellow as that carbon copy.

Chapter 6

What's in The American Sublime?

We pulled into one of the massive parking lots along the stretch of beaches that had fire pits. We got out and grabbed the boards. Tommy, Lee, and Jessie had rushed past me and were quickly out in the water. But I wanted to take this moment in, as when my parents got back, I might be on restriction for the rest of my life; that is if they let me live. But it's too late now. What's done is done, might as well just enjoy this moment.

The sand was warm between my toes. The stained salt air mixed with the smells of overused firepits. As I approached the water, my confidence waned. The roar and pounding of each wave vibrated right through me. My heartbeat quickened with each step. The sun danced and shimmered all over every ripple in the water. It was magical.

The board I had, stood much taller than me and was awkward, at best, to carry. The seagulls constantly vied for prime spots of left-over trash, picking over the remains of whatever they could find. The sand was denser the closer I got to the water.

I left the hot sand and walked on the much cooler wet sand, increased my pace, and jumped into knee-deep water. The cold of the ocean hit me like a ton of bricks, knocking the wind out of me. I watched the water rush away from under my feet. I walked further out. Now the water was waist-high.

Ribbons from a butterfly kite caught my attention. It danced on the air tethered to a young boy standing on the shore with his dad. Wham! A wave crashed into my back, knocking me off my feet. The extended rubber leash that tethered me to my board pulled me under the water. I tumbled around and around, over and over again.

I had no idea what was up or down. Soon fear overcame me. Sounds were muted, strangely echoey, and rushing in from every angle. All I wanted to do was breathe. It was dark and then light, dark, then light again. I could see a blurred image of the sky and push up with everything I had. When my head bobbed out of the water, I gasped for air. Along with it, I ingested a healthy amount of salty, sandy water.

A wave crashed over my head. I was sucked under, twirling like a top, my shoulders slammed into the sandy bottom. I dog paddled the best I could, but the current was too strong. In a panic, I reached for the leash I was tethered to. I grabbed it and pulled with every bit of energy I had left.

I reached the surface of the water and clung to my board like glue. I had no idea where I was. The pier was much smaller. I was way further out than I could have imagined being, and I didn't see anyone I recognized.

I kicked my feet, pointing the board in the direction of the shore. I sneezed, and there was as much sand coming out of my nose as there was snot. I got back into the waves, and they pushed me faster to the shore. One crashed over me, I closed my eyes, and I held the board as tight as I could as the wave twirled me around.

It stopped, I opened my eyes and road the whitewash into shore. I actually kissed the sand when I made it in and gave silent thanks to God that I was still alive. I got up and figured I had at least a couple of miles or so to walk to get back to the others.

***

I passed these two beautiful girls on the way back to the bus in the parking lot. Both college age, one had a pink duffel bag and surfboard, very Barbie-like. The other girl had an Indian style bag and tie-dyed board. She was someone my mom would have referred to as an earth muffin.

I overheard one of them asking for some cash for a bus ticket. I only remembered that because it seemed like a reasonable request to me, but the guys they were talking to ignored them and left. I personally thought it was kind of rude. They could have at least said they didn't have any money.

I got back to the bus after what felt to be forever. Strangely, no one asked where I had been. Tommy and Lee were pulling camping stuff out of the bus until I pointed out a sign posted on the wall near the parking lot.

The sign said: Beach closes at 10pm No overnight camping. Tommy sighed and stuffed the gear back on the bus.

Lee pulled out a cigarette, lit it, and looked at Jessie, "Nice parking."

"I didn't see where it said, 'NO overnight parking.' Chill already."

"Hey, you owe me a month of no smoking," I said.

"Really?" he retorted, but his rebuttal was interrupted by the two beautiful girls I saw earlier approaching us.

Lee elbowed Tommy, "Hot Bettys, twelve O'clock!"

I looked at my watch, confused. It was nowhere near twelve O'clock. When I looked back up, the two girls were standing with us next to Jessie's V.W. bus.

The earth muffin greeted us with a simple, "Hey."

The other one quickly followed with, "Could I bum a cigarette?"

Lee fumbled over his words and finally squeaked out a, "Sure."

She thanked him with a smile and took a cigarette out of Lee's red-topped Marlboro pack. He and Tommy looked at me like they just won the lottery. The two girls stood on either side of me.

The earthy one, even though she smelled nice and looked clean, appeared to have never washed her hair. But the look worked for her, and I found myself strangely attracted to her. But then I compared her to Sally and afterward thought she wasn't that great.

She said, "I'm June and this is April."

Tommy blurted out, "Those are my favorite months."

"Jess," said Jessie.

"Lee," said Lee.

"Ben," I said.

Tommy deepened his voice and said, "I'm Tom." We all looked at Tommy like; you've never referred to yourself like that before. He looked back at us and said, "What?" It was clear he thought he had a chance with one of these girls, but it was pretty apparent to me that they were there just there to milk us for a few dollars.

June, "Nice boards. Get any good ones today?"

"No, I couldn't get up," I said.

Lee and Tommy lost it, laughing. With that, Jessie then lost it with them. I didn't get was so funny at the time, but back then, I was a little naïve. I take that back. I'm still a little naïve. At least that's what my wife tells me, and a wise husband never argues with his wife. Anyway, I wasn't buying into their little act at all and was ready to walk like the guys I saw earlier did. June looked at me, seductively.

"I bet you just need more stimulating waves." She said as she slid her hand up my back, and I have to say it felt quite amazing. Lee and Tommy dropped their jaws and looked like they couldn't believe what they were seeing. I knew it was all an act and was becoming more and more irritated, these two girls were sucking the life out of what could have been a good time. I kept hoping they would just leave.

Jessie looked at June and April and asked, "You guys catch any?"

June replied, "A few, there's nothing that special here."

"No doubt, everything was blown out," April said, "We were on our way to grab some waves in Mushrooms, but our car crapped out, and this is far as we got bumming rides. Can you spare any bus money?"

"Mushrooms?" Tommy asked. This was when I knew they had to be full of shit. As much as Tommy loved surfing, there was no way he wouldn't know about a surfable beach nearby.

"Totally, we plan on hitting up T.J. for a party and then Mushrooms for some real sick waves," said June.

"T.J.? Isn't that like in Mexico?" Tommy asked. There were times I wondered if Tommy had a brain at all. You couldn't help but to like the guy, but it always felt like he was two steps behind everybody, and his grades were as good as mine. How was that even possible?

April jumped in, "Yeah, like there are breaks that go for like a mile. Waves at Mushrooms are like wicked."

"Never heard of it," Tommy said.

Something didn't sit right with these girls. They started to feel more like the pushy panhandlers we used to walk by in San Francisco when we'd go visit my grandma.

June told Tommy, "Just south of Rosarito is a funky leaning tower. Anyway, most people never pay any attention to it. And it's right next to this beach that no one ever really goes to or knows about. That's Mushrooms. One of the best surfing spots in all of Baja."

All I could think was that these two gals had had one too many mushrooms themselves. I did know about those drugs we had a whole class on them in health ed after a couple kids went to the E.R. for sniffing glue.

"Yeah, if you love surfing, it's a must," April said.

"Totally!" June said, "The waves at Mushrooms are killer. They are what set it apart from any other spot in Baja."

"What are the waves like?" Tommy asked.

"Head high to double overhead high on an average day," June answered.

"Totally!" April jumped in, "Last time we were there, they were triple overhead high."

I was now waiting for a triple dog dare you, like from a Christmas Story. This conversation was becoming painful. I was getting ready to ask how much money they wanted so they would shut up and go away.

"A beach with waves that big, and no one around snaking your waves just isn't easy to find in Mexico," June added.

"Or anywhere else in the world," Tommy said.

"Exactly." April said, "And it's only like three hours to get there once you cross the border."

"That's it?" Tommy asked, "We're only like three hours away from some of the best beaches in the world?"

"Yep, well five if you count getting to the border." June answered, "Just take the last Rosarito exit at Pernex Station and turn left. The beach is about four miles down the road. It's easy to spot because of the funky pink tower."

This magical place they were talking about was too far-fetched to be true. I couldn't believe how these girls had Tommy and Lee completely mesmerized. Me, on the other hand, I had had all I could take.

I said, "How much do you need for the bus?"

Lee chimed in, "Hey, we should just take them."

Jessie and I looked at each other like he was nuts. I was glad to see I had at least one person that might be on my side for this one. I definitely did not want to go to Mexico.

"Ah! We are like not all over 18, never get over the border." Jessie said.

But June came back with, "They only like check the ID of the driver and most times they don't even check and wave you through. I could drive us over the border... that is if you wanna go?"

"To Mexico? I asked in shock, "No way!"

"That would be totally cool, and save us a bus ticket," said June.

"Wow, you're so sweet," April said to me.

It was definitely not meant to be sweet, and it pissed me off that she took it that way, knowing damn well what I expected.

Jessie followed with, "I don't think so, I'm not cool with anyone driving my ride…"

I didn't waste a second and said, "Second that."

"Come on, it would be bad!" Lee said.

"Now, that would be the endless summer!" Tommy proclaimed.

With hesitation, Jessie stuck to, "I don't know, I'm not feeling it."

The waver in Jessie's voice sent a cold chill down my spine, I didn't like that he was starting to waver.

"If we left now, we could be over the border in like two hours." June said, followed by April, "Totally, and like there won't be anyone to wait in line behind."

Tommy and Lee looked at Jessie with begging eyes. Jessie gave in and nodded his head.

"Yes!" Tommy and Lee shouted in unison.

"Nice, mind if we change on the road?" April asked.

Tommy and Lee blurt out, "Yes! We, I mean no. Like sure, change."

***

Lee and Tommy were in the back of the bus with June and April. I was in the front passenger seat, pulling my journal from my backpack. The ocean was no longer visible cause it was so dark. And there wasn't anything other than white lines on the road to look at. I wrote, you know, things just seem to escalate when you start lying. In less than twenty-four hours, I had stolen my dad's credit card, committed grand larceny, watched two girls get naked, and was now headed for another country.

I stopped writing as it started to make me nauseous. I looked at Jessie, who seemed agitated and I said, "Sorry,"

"For what?" He asked.

"Just sucks chemo isn't working for your dad. I complain that my dad's never around, but I can't imagine losing him." I said.

"Yeah." He said.

"I always wished my dad was like him."

"Really?"

"Yeah," I said, "I mean, he was a cool coach." He was, too, talk about a guy that made sure everyone followed the rules. He gave out push-ups if you were late, if you goofed off or were generally disrespectful in any way. He was my favorite part of playing baseball and quite possibly the thing I missed the most.

"I thought everyone hated him." He said.

"Why, because he made us work?" I asked.

Jessie laughed, "We did take first that year. What made you think of that?"

"Just wanted you to know, that's all."

"You're pretty cool, you know?" He said.

"You think?" I asked, he nodded, and I said, "Thanks."

V.W. busses don't have the best shocks in the world. In fact, I'm not sure they have any at all. I mean, you feel every single bump in the road. Most times, it's no big deal. Most of the time, riding in them is pretty cool, all the windows and space, but once your body sends you a signal that your bladder is full, feeling all those bumps in the road is torture. You have no choice, you have to go like right away.

"Hey," I said, "I got to go. Mind pulling over?"

"I gotta go too." Jessie said, "I'll hit the next station."

I looked and the tag that Jessie had written the last mileage on, it was only 30 miles different. So, I asked, "You got to go one or two?"

"One."

"Why don't we just stop on the side and—"

"No. We'll stop at a station!" He said.

"OK."

I swear I was about to pee myself, every little bump made me feel like I was about to leak a few drops out. The V.W. bus finally pulled into a station. Lee, Tommy, April, and June stayed in the bus while Jessie and I made a beeline into the station.

Typically, I would never have entered such a disgusting bathroom, but I had to go so bad I didn't care. There were two johns and an enclosed toilet. I hit the one next to the enclosed toilet. I unzipped and let it go. It actually hurt coming out, because I waited so long.

Jessie passed by the empty john and went into the enclosed toilet. Why anyone would want to enter any further into this cesspool of germs was beyond me. I looked down and saw Jessie's shorts around his ankles. I only heard the sound of peeing, a tissue tear, and flush.

I zipped up a little confused. I walked to the sink. The water was so cold when it hit my hands, it caused my jaw to lock up. I pushed the dispenser for soap, but no surprise, nothing came out. Jessie joined me briefly and left.

On the way out of the bathroom, I spotted a rack of Thomas Guides. I grabbed one, along with some sanitizing soap, and went to the counter.

Back at the bus, Jessie opened his door only to find June sitting in the driver seat. I climbed into the passenger side.

"Mind if I take over?" June asked.

Jessie replied, "Sure, no, go ahead." And got in the back with Lee, Tommy, and April.

***

The V.W. bus pulled into the border station. June looked at me and said, "Pretend you're asleep."

"Yeah. Act like you're asleep." April followed.

A border patrol guy with fiery red hair, pockmarks that could rival a pizza, and DAVE embordered on his uniform waved to June.

She shouted, "Dave!"

Dave got all excited. He looked like a total dweeb. All I could hope was that I never looked like that. He leaned into the window and tried to act all cool. "Hey," his voice cracked, "June, right?"

June smiled at him, I knew that smile, my uncle used it all the time when he was conning someone. She looked around, pulled a bag from her purse, and handed it to him.

He looked in the bag and smiled, “Nice. Go on through.”

“You gonna party with us in T.J.?” She said to him.

“Maybe. OK, get out of here before the shift change.”

She winked at him and drove us over the border.

Chapter 7

Where's the Dinner Bell in the Woods?

I still couldn't believe I was in another country without my mom and dad. I was flipping out inside. It was worse than that wave that kicked my ass. This was the kind of shit you heard about on the ten o'clock news. Stupid teens get killed in Mexico for being dumb asses. Like that idiotic show, *When Animals Attack*, that should have been named when stupid people get bit. And right about now, I was feeling like one of those 'stupid' people.

April wasn't nearly as pretty as Sally, no one was. And I didn't want to look when they were changing, but Lee called me, and when I looked, there she was in her birthday suit. It was hard to look at her now without thinking about it. Plus, it may sound silly, but I was kind of hoping the first girl I'd see that way was Sally. I get it, never going to happen, right? But dreaming is free, and we all have is our issues. I thought about how I could take Sally's name, so I would be Ben Rhodes instead of Ben Dover. Wasn't that much better, but hey, beggars can't be choosers.

The road we got on turned off the main highway. The area we were driving into got creepier and creepier the longer we were on it. This place made Lee's house look like a mansion. Shady wouldn't begin to describe the rat's nest we were heading into.

We came to a shack, well, a poorly kept two-story house that looked like it survived one too many wars. A lot of very drunk half-clothed college-age kids littered the front lawn. The most anyone was wearing was some underwear. A bunch of them were passed out on the spotty dirt field that surrounded the shack; others were heaving up stuff in the corners.

Lee and Tommy looked like someone just told them they won the lottery, even Jessie was looking more excited. April parked the bus.

"We're here!" she said.

"You're welcome to come party if you want," said June.

"Cha!" Tommy retorted.

Lee's mood shifted, and he became increasingly uneasy. He spotted what he thought were two federales sitting in cars at the corner. When I looked at what he was looking at, I didn't see federales. I saw what two tatted-up dudes armed with machine guns. They looked more like the mafia than cops. April and June got out of the bus and grabbed their stuff.

"You coming?" June asked.

"Hey, I need to talk to my friends first," Lee answered.

"Cool." June said, followed by April, saying, "See you inside." The two girls walked off utterly unphased by all the partying around them.

"I'm on the fence," Jessie said.

"What!" Tommy said.

"We need to get the hell out of here!" Lee said.

"Wait! What? Dude, buzzkill!" Tommy said.

Lee pointed to the corner where the federales were. We all watched as another one pulled up to the other corner of the house.

"I think we better get out of here," Lee said.

"Second that," Tommy said.

Jessie hopped into the front seat and started the bus and said, "Where the hell are we—"

"Just drive!" we all said.

The V.W. bus pulled out. Another couple of mafia-type federales passed by us. Tommy watched and said, "Okay, I take it back. That would've been the buzzkill."

Jessie was panicking, "Now what do we do? I have no clue where we are?"

"Hold on," I said. I pulled out the Thomas Guide and found the street where we were. I pointed on the map so that Jessie could see.

"I think we are here. So, if we follow this road, it should take us to Emiliano Zapata, when we get there, turn left, it should take us to the one highway."

Lee smiled, "That's my boy."

"Yeah, all MacGyver and shit," Tommy added.

***

Jessie sped down the road. I remember thinking the worst was behind us. We had decided to continue to Mushrooms, since we had already come this far. Lee and Tommy were sacked out in the back, they both snored. Jessie and I shared a laugh about it. I looked out the window and the open road in front of us. It was empty, not like at home, there was no such thing as an empty highway regardless of the hour. It was kind of cool to look out for miles and see nothing but road.

I sat there wondering, head spinning with random thoughts as it often does. I mean, why were two hot girls, way out of our league, remotely interested in us? Then I recalled the bag she handed the guy at the border. I've never been a hundred percent sure of what was in it, but it was a good bet that you could add drug running to my laundry list of felonies for the day.

***

Jessie drove along a stretch of highway filled with bluffs. The sky turned from dark midnight to bright red. I couldn't help but fixate on the saying red sky in the morning sailor take warning, red sky at night sailors delight. Tommy looked out the window. His eyes went wide.

"Dude!" he yelled out, "Check out those waves! Pullover!"

Jessie pulled over on this steep hill, nose facing down. I looked at him like, are you sure this is a good idea? He pulled the hand brake and gave me an, I got this look. Then it slid back a little, and then I gave him an, are you sure look. And he gave me what I think was an, I'm pretty sure look.

We stood outside the bus holding our boards looking down the bluff and at each other. Silently saying with our eyes, "How the hell are we going to get down there?"

Tommy pointed, "Look." There was this narrow path that looked like with careful navigation, we could almost make it safely to the beach below.

About halfway down, a grinding sound could be heard from above.

Lee stepped on a sharp rock and squealed and pleaded, "Hey, stop!"

"Why?" Tommy asked.

"It's killing my feet!"

"Pansy," Jessie said.

"Bite me!"

I heard the grinding sound again, but it was louder, "Did you hear that?" I asked.

"Yeah, he's a pansy." Tommy retorted.

"You can bite me too!" Lee said.

Tommy laughed and said, "man up already."

There were more grinding noises. It sounded like it was coming from the V.W. bus. "There it is again," I said.

"What?" Tommy asked.

"That weird noise!" I said.

"You're tripping, man," Tommy said, still laughing.

The grinding ended abruptly, followed by a loud clank and the sound of the bus rolling down the hill. We looked up to see the unmanned bus racing down the mountain. In unison, we all said, "Oh, crap!"

Chapter 8

Do we sink or swim In a Bad Time?

I pointed to where the bus was headed, "Over there!"

The road followed the bluff down a hill where it ended at a sandy beach. About a half-mile down the shoreline from where we were.

Jessie yelled, "Come on! Go, Go, Go!"

We all kicked it into a new gear hurrying down the rocky bluff to the sand below. Tommy, Jessie, and Lee dropped their boards and bolted off after the bus. I followed close behind.

Lee turned, looked at me, and said, "Stay with the boards!"

I stopped and watched the others sprint away down the beach, jumping over and scrambling through the terrain. I sighed, feeling left out a little and walked back to the boards. Although awkward, I was able to pick up and carry all four boards. I headed down the beach at a speeded-up walk.

The VW bus hit loose gravel at the bottom of the hill where the road curved. The back end spun towards the beach as it rocketed onto the sand. The bus slid about 100 yards into the soft sand before stopping. That's when the others caught up to it.

Honestly, I don't know why we were running; it's not like any of us could have stopped it. But then again, when the adrenaline is pumping, the brain is often disengaged.

Carrying four surfboards started out easy, but man, they got heavy. About halfway to the V.W., I felt like my arms were going to fall off. I tried dragging them, but that was even worse. It felt like it would be forever before I reached them. As I walked, I was debating how this was fun in any way, shape, or form. And why the hell didn't any of them come back and help me? It was just like last summer, all uncle John had me do was tote his luggage and run errands for him. Aside from counting cards, it was a horrible summer. And here I was again, hauling other people's shit around.

"Oh crap, not good," said Jessie.

"Totally," said Tommy.

Lee nodded and said, "How long you think it would take to get it out?"

"No clue. Maybe we just camp here tonight," Jessie said.

"Look at the bright side." Said Tommy as he looked out at the ocean and smiled. "The waves look great. Grab your board!"

We all looked at Tommy like he was on crack. He gave us a 'What' type of look and saw I had his board.

"Sweet!" He said. And with that, he grabbed his board and headed for the waves. Lee and Jessie looked at each other, shrugged their shoulders, grabbed their boards, and head for the waves as well.

Dream On

"Come on, dude!" Lee shouted back at me.

I grabbed my board and hoped for a better wave than the last one that pulled me under.

Once I got past the shells and rocks, the powdered white sand felt good on my feet. It wasn't coarse like the sand was in Huntington or Newport, but more powdery; almost dirt-like. The water shimmered and sparkled with bright blueish turquoise. It was so clear. I hadn't seen anything like it. Plus, we were the only ones on the beach. Making it feel even more surreal and magical. My negative thoughts dissipated.

I ran through a giant water spot that the whitewash had left behind. Oh, man! Now that was a real pain! I had no clue jellyfish got that big.

"My foot!" I yelled. I looked down, and there it was the biggest figging jellyfish I'd ever seen. Its tentacles had whipped around my foot and ankle.

"Jellyfish!" I screamed. I was doing everything I could do not to fall on the damn thing. I stood there, balancing on the one foot that was planted dead center of the jellyfish. I wanted to set my other foot back down, but I couldn't see a way to do that without setting on another part of that massive thing.

My foot was burning so bad. I could see red bumps developing on my skin right before my eyes, I almost passed out.

Lee got to me first and steadied me, so I didn't have to put my other foot down.

"Help?" was all I could utter.

Lee looked down, seeing my foot turning redder by the second and said, "OH! Shit, dude!"

Tommy got there soon after, "We got you!" Tommy said, "Lift your foot up slowly."

They held me up. I lifted my foot off, and between the saltwater and the cold air, the sting intensified. I couldn't help it; I couldn't hold back the tears. I don't know what hurt worse, the pain of the jellyfish or the bruised pride I was feeling from balling my eyes out.

Jessie caught up to us just as Lee and Tommy had cleared me away from the jellyfish. Tommy looked at Jessie and said, "Quick! Pee on his foot!"

Lee looked at him like he was nuts and said, "What!?"

Followed quickly with Jessie saying, "What!?"

"It will kill the sting, trust me!" Tommy said.

"He's right, do it!" I said. I've been told since then that peeing on your foot to kill the sting of a jellyfish is a myth. I'm here to tell you it does help. I don't care what anyone says, someone steps on a jellyfish, pee on them!

"I can't!" Jessie said.

"Come on! We can't hold him forever!" Lee said.

The sting got more intense along with my crying. The pain was so overwhelming that I no longer cared about my pride.

Tommy looked at Jessie and said, "Come on, already!"

"I can't!" Jessie insisted.

Tommy held me up with one arm, dropped his pants, and peed on my foot. I watched Jessie, had no choice really, he was right in front of me. Jessie looked totally embarrassed when Tommy dropped his pants. In fact, Jessie turned away supper fast and then peeked at Tommy's tool like he'd never seen one before.

Tommy and Lee helped me sit to the ground, and Jessie looked just like my cousin Steve after he got caught looking at my uncle Fred's Playboys.

After a long period of silence, Lee looked at my foot, "You OK?" I nodded, and he continued, "Mind if we hit some waves?"

I shook my head. And asked, “Mind getting my backpack for me first. Lee shook his head and left for the bus. Tommy and Jessie picked up their boards, and this time, instead of running out onto the shoreline, they carefully navigate it.

Lee left his board next to me and sprinted to the bus. When he got there, he grabbed my backpack. But that wasn't it. I watched as he lugged a cooler and an umbrella as well. When he got back to me, he said, "Forgot to ask if you wanted something to drink. So I just brought you everything."

I said, "Dude." and gave him a thumbs up.

He smiled, opened the umbrella, angled it to shade me from the sun, and slammed it into the ground. He simply smiled at me, then grabbed his board and headed out for the waves avoiding my jellyfish.

I opened my backpack and pulled out my journal. I knew exactly what I had planned on writing before Lee got my stuff. But now I had no clue. Although my foot was still throbbing, the pain wasn't all that bad. Especially with Lee being so chill. He was definitely an enigma and wasn't sure how to feel about him. I thought the jellyfish was just par for the coarse but, then again, would I have ever seen that side of Lee without it?

Anyway, I still was pondering Jessie's reaction to Tommy. Maybe he liked guys, of course, with this group that would definitely be something to hide. But if he was turned on, how did he not have a hard-on? I mean, his shorts were totally wet. Something didn't add up.

I missed my house, my room, and my desk. The light there was perfect for writing in a journal. I didn't have to fight the glare of the sun or wipe sand off the paper. I looked down at the blank pages of the journal and realized I was stuck in my head and hadn't written a thing.

Tommy rode up the side of a beautifully shaped wave and jumped into the air, making it look so easy. I could see why Tommy liked surfing so much, it was like he could fly. I envied the freedom he must have felt.

Jessie popped up on his board and managed to stay up. He wiped out when he tried to cut back into the wave but quickly resurfaced cheering.

Lee pushed water in Jessie's face. He still hadn't stayed up on a wave. Jessie flipped him off. His hair fell around his face, and from a distance, he looked strangely attractive as he climbed back on his board. I noticed that Jessie had a different shape then Lee and Tommy. He looked like he might even have, wait! I finally knew It! Jessie's a girl, he had to be. Guys don't have hips like that.

Lee came out of the water and sat next to me. It was a nice break in the solitude I was enjoying.

"Isn't this great?" He said.

"I don't know. If I was honest, part of me wants to go back home."

"How's the foot?" Lee asked.

"Sore, but not as bad."

"Guess that's one of those times where it's better to be pissed on than pissed off." He said.

We shared a laugh, and I asked, "Why do you think Jessie was so weird about peeing on my foot?"

Lee laughed and said, "He's always had issues, don't let it bother you. What're you writin'?

"Just my thoughts about things."

"Let me see."

"No, it's personal," I said.

Lee grabbed the journal from my hands, and my heart sank.

"Hey! Give it back!" I yelled.

"Chill!" Lee said as he looked through the journal. "That's messed up, someone really put you headfirst in the trash?" He asked.

I nodded.

"I thought wedgies just happen in bad teen movies." He said.

I shook my head and thought about how Miguel gave me wedgies almost every day after lunch. That was, of course, before Lee. After we became friends, nobody messed with me.

"Can I have it back please?" I asked.

Lee flipped another page and read, he stopped smiling and looked like he had stumbled on to a hidden treasure. "That's bad! Dude. Your uncle taught you how to count cards? That's sick."

"Yeah. Uncle John is pretty cool. You'd like him." I said.

Lee continued to read. “Wow, Really?" Lee asked. He paused and was silent. I hadn't seen this side of him. For a moment, he seemed vulnerable. He looked at me and sincerely said, "I'm the first friend you've ever had?"

I nodded.

We stared at each other for a moment. I looked out to the ocean where Tommy and Jessie played in the surf. With a deep breath, I let out, "You, Tommy, and Jessie are the only friends I've ever had."

"Didn't you ever have any birthday parties or anything growing up?” Lee asked.

"Yeah, my mom invited a bunch of kids over for my 7th birthday, but they ended up beating me up. It was awful. My mom had to step in and everything. It was the worst birthday ever." I said.

Lee got a surprised expression on his face. He looked at me like something was wrong with what I wrote.

"Wait? You think Jessie's a girl?" He asked.

"I don't know. Now, give it back!" I said.

I tried snatching the journal back, but Lee kept it just out of my reach. He shook his head and returned to his usual demeanor. Lee looked at me. I could see it in his face. He was still waiting for an answer to his last question. All I could come up with was, "They're just random thoughts. That's why you're not supposed to look in other people's journals!" It was kind of lame but still honest.

"I like you,” he said, “But you're wack sometimes."

"Can I have my journal back, please?" I asked yet again.

He finally handed me back my journal.

Chapter 9

A Hibiscus on the Sleeping Shores?

The blue of the ocean could still be seen at night even after the sun had long since set. It would have been perfect if we didn't have to put up with the stench of burning plastic.

Jessie must have been able to read my mind. He looked at Lee and said, "I told you the plastic crap on the pallet needed to be pulled off first."

"But it makes cool colors, man," Lee said.

"It reeks!" Jessie said.

“I second that,” I said.

Tommy shruged his shoulders, puts some chips in his mouth, and said with a mouth full of chips, “I'm with Lee, I like the cool colors man.” Tommy pointed at Lee and said, "Truth or dare?"

Lee's grin didn't quite make it to his cheek before answering, "Dare."

Tommy swallowed the last bit of chips and took a bite of his hot dog. Still chewing on the dog, he said, "I dare you to... pick your nose and eat it."

"Oh, that's nasty!" I said.

Jessie chimed in, "Grody!"

Lee looked at Tommy. “Are you serious? If so, not cool.” At least that was the look Lee gave Tommy.

Tommy laughed. A mix of over-chewed chips and some hotdog escaped his mouth. "Come on. Do it!" He said. Tommy’s laughter was infectious, and even though this was grossing me out, I couldn’t stop myself from laughing.

Lee slowly put his middle finger in his nose, pointing at Tommy and grinned, pulling it out, flipping him off. He slowly moved his tongue to the dangling yellow slime at the tip of his dirty nail and quickly licked his finger. I felt my stomach turn, mainly as I knew these games only escalated.

"Oh, man." I let out.

Tommy laughed even harder, "No way."

"Barf me out," Jessie said.

I laughed so hard I almost peed myself. Lee looks right at me, almost through me. I could see the wheels turning in his head, and my laughter soon turned to fear.

"Ben, truth, or dare?" Lee said.

"I don't know why we call this truth or dare. We only ever do dares." Jessie said.

For a brief moment, I thought it was over, and Jessie’s boredom with the game would get me out of the hot seat. Lee laughed, but it was evil. He looked at me like he did when he read my journal. My heart was thumping in my throat. It was worse than how I felt cheating for Sally. He continued staring at me. Lee laughed, but it was an evil type of laugh.

"OK," Lee said, "I dare you to ask Jessie truth or dare, and when he picks truth, ask him what we talked about earlier."

"Go for it," Jessie said.

"This ought to be good," said Tommy.

"No way," I said, "I told you that was-"

"Dude!" Tommy interrupted, "Just ask him."

I didn't have time to form a well-rehearsed response, so I just sat there trying to think of a way out of this.

"Yeah! Just ask, 'him,'" Lee said, laughing, "Come on, dude!"

"Fine, truth, or dare?" I asked.

Jessie replied, "Truth."

I looked with pleading eyes to Lee, "Do I have to?"

"Don't wuss out!" he said.

I knew further delay would just piss everyone off. I wiped the sweat from my brow, knowing if I was wrong, I was going to get the crap beat out of me. And with a deep sigh, I asked, "Are you a girl?"

Tommy choked on his hotdog, and Jessie's face went pale. I could actually feel Jessie's stomach turn. Lee could barely form words through his sinister laugh.

"He had this idea that you weren't a guy. I told him he was whack." Lee said.

Tommy cut me down with a disapproving look and said, "Not cool."

I retorted, "Well, he wouldn't pee on my foot or change with anyone in sight. He has cramps once a month, and he still hasn't answered the question."

Lee buried his head in his hands and said, "Jessie, would you please set his head straight."

Tommy interrupted, "He makes a good point, only one way to know for sure."

"I am not dropping my pants for you guys!" Jessie whipped.

"You don't have to," I said.

"Yeah, just pull your shorts really tight," Lee said, "and make sure it's pointing up."

Lee and Tommy both laughed at me, but Jessie was not amused. In fact, he was near tears. He shook his head, reluctantly. Tears welled and slowly made tracks through the beach residue on his cheeks.

"Dude, it's not that bad," Lee said.

"I'm not a dude," Jessie said.

"It's OK. Wait, what?!" Lee questioned.

"What did he just say?" Tommy asked.

I had no clue I just opened a massive can of worms. And my curiosity got in the way of what should have been compassion as I continued asking, "Why did you pretend to be a guy?"

Jessie looked down and said, "I wanted to play baseball, not softball, and so I lied and said I was a guy. Then we became friends, and I didn't want to be treated different cause I was a girl."

"Jessie's a Betty?" Tommy asked, still in shock, trying to process the information.

"Dude, catch up," Lee said.

"Does your dad know?" Tommy asked.

Lee and I looked at Tommy like he was an idiot.

She nodded, "He knew," Jessie said, "He knew how bad I wanted to play baseball and..."

"Lying, so you don't have to own up, isn't cool!" Lee yelled.

Jessie glared at all of us, her anger swelling, she looked at me and yelled, "Yeah. Sure! Like you would have ever asked me to play catch." she looked at Tommy and said, "Or upgrade bearings on your wheels." And then she looked at Lee and said, "Or spring load your knife if I was a 'Betty'!"

"How would you know?!" Lee yelled back, "You never gave us that chance! I stood up for you when Ben said you were a girl, I trusted you."

"I'm still the same person," she said.

"No! Lee yelled, "No, you're not. You're a girl." He motioned to his crotch and continued, "We are physically different!"

"Like, she totally saw my..." Tommy looks down at his crotch, then looked at Jessie.

"Sorry, I didn't mean to," Jessie said.

"This is so gnarly," Tommy added.

"Didn't mean to what?!" Lee yelled, "Lie to us? 'Cause you totally meant to do that."

"Look, when we met, everyone already thought I was a guy," Jessie said.

"That makes it OK?" Lee quipped, "Lying to get whatever you want?"

"It's not like that," said Jessie.

"Isn't that what you did?" said Lee. "You wanted to play ball, and you lied, so you got yours."

"Dude!" Tommy said to Lee, "Dial it down a notch."

Jessie yelled at Lee, "Do you have any idea what it's like to live with a label! And not get to do things because of it!"

"Yes!" Lee yelled back at her, "Yes, I do! Try doing anything after going to juvie. You're always labeled the bad kid, but if any of you couldn't deal with that, then I didn't care, because real friends don't lie to each other! They either got your back or not!" Lee stood, shook his head, and stopped whatever he had planned on saying and just said, "Dude," and walked away.

He walked along the shore, picking up things and throwing them into the ocean on his way back to the bus. I was about to get up, then Jessie let out a mournful sigh.

“I’m, I’m sorry you guys.” We didn’t know what to say. She continued, "Just adds to the point."

"What point?" I asked.

"If I can't fool you guys, how will I ever fool the military?"

"Now I am totally lost," said Tommy.

"I always dreamed of being a fighter pilot like my dad, but they don't let girls do that," said Jessie.

"I'm pretty sure that the first time you hit the showers, they'd figure it out," Tommy said.

"Yeah," I added, "how were you going to pull that off?"

“I didn't say I had it worked out!” She said.

“Lee has a point,” I said, “We’re still here because we like you, not because you're a girl or guy.

“True. But he's wiggin.” Jessie said.

Lee slammed the slider on the bus shut. We all turned and looked in his direction.

I asked, “Think he'll be OK?”

“Who? Lee?” Tommy asked, “Yep, he's just hot-headed.”

Chapter 10

What's the Anecdote of the Jar?

Just for the record, I hate camping. Whoever thought it was a great idea to sleep in a nylon-bag, on hard ground, out in the elements should be shot. I woke up with sand stuck to half my face. It was everywhere, sand that is. Not to mention the stink from the plastic coming out of the fire pit next to me was ten times worse. I wanted a hot shower, warm pop tarts, and a cozy couch to wake up on while I watched Scooby-Doo. Unfortunately, I was in the middle of nowhere without any modern conveniences. And so far, I hated surfing.

It didn't help that the morning started off with another yelling match between Lee and Jessie. I lost track of who said the meanest things, didn't matter really, they were both acting like idiots.

Tommy and I tried to ignore them and hoped they'd come to their senses. Tommy thought he'd bring us all together by suggesting getting the V.W. unstuck. Not a bad idea really, and it did get the two of them to be at least civil for a little bit.

Jessie sat in the driver's seat, started the motor, and put her foot on the gas pedal. The tires spun in the sand, but the V.W. bus didn't budge. Tommy and Lee looked at me like well? I thought for a moment, then remembered this equation from physics class.

"Great, now what?" Tommy asked.

"We-"I started.

Lee interrupted, "Dude, just jump up and down in the back and hit the reverse."

"Um, like no," Jessie said.

"We need to dig the tires out," I said.

"This bites!" Tommy said.

"I agree with Ben," Jessie said.

Lee ignored Jessie's presence, he never made eye contact with her, not once. He said to Tommy, "Did you hear something?"

Tommy replied in a way that meant enough is enough already.

Lee looked at me, "We'll dig this side out."

Lee and I used our hands and dug out a trench on the passenger's side back tire as Jessie and Tommy dug out a channel on the driver's side rear tire.

I was kind of in my element and was enjoying digging in the sand, weird, right? It reminded me of when I was a kid… OK, a younger kid, playing with hot wheels in the sandbox and digging tunnels for them. I got so into it, I felt like a foreman or something and said, "You want to dig down until you can see the bottom of your tire." I pointed to the road and continued, "And we need to scoop out a trench in that direction."

"No shit, Sherlock." Lee said. I could always trust Lee to tell it to me straight. And I had a tendency to be a bit condescending, so he was perfect for me.

"Take a chill pill." Jessie said.

"Did you hear anything?" Lee asked.

"What's your damage?" Tommy asked.

Jessie shook her head and got in the bus. It was weird calling Jessie a 'her.' It took me a long time to get used to it. Lee looked at Tommy and shook his head, "I don't do posers."

Jessie walked off. She got in the bus and started it.

"Not yet!" I yelled. The trench was only part one.

She must not have heard me or didn't care, but she floored it, spinning the tires in the sand again. The V.W. rocked a little but got stuck. Jessie turned off the engine.

Lee looked at me and spouted, "Now what, genius?"

"Chill already, man!" Tommy yelled.

"We need to let the air out of tires before we try and get it out," I said.

Tommy looked at me and said, "Dude? You're trippin?"

"No, it will create a greater surface area," I said, "Now that we've dug the sand out around the tire-"

Lee cut me off again, "That's my boy. Deadly, dude MacGyver." At least this time, it seemed like he gave me a compliment before he cut me off. Lee and Tommy removed the caps from the tires and pressed the release.

"How much?" Tommy asked.

"Let about a quarter of the air pressure out," I said.

"Good?" Tommy asked.

"Yeah," I said.

"How about mine?" Lee asked.

"Should be good," I said. This is where book smarts get tested. I prayed it would work, or it would be the last time anyone here listened to me.

"Punch it, Jess!" Tommy yelled.

"No!" I yelled, "Not yet. We need the floor mats out of the van."

"Bus!" Jessie corrected.

"No, prob dude, we'll get the mats out of the 'van,'" Lee said.

Jessie shook her head. Under her breath, she said, "I'm gonna leave him here. I swear I'll leave 'em all friggin here. She must have seen the look of panic on my face and said, "Not you. I need you to get home."

Lee and Tommy look at each other like what the heck and grab the mats out of the van. I told them to take the floor mats and flip them upside down, so the rubber bottom is facing upwards. And stick them under the tires to give it a better surface for traction.

Lee said, "Tight."

"Yes," I said, "make sure they are in tight."

The three of them laughed at me. I found that, more often than not, I was missing the meanings of their expressions.

Lee and Tommy put the mats under the tires.

"All good," Tommy said.

I pointed to the front of the bus and said, "Tommy, you and Lee need to go to the front of the bus and push." They both dashed up to the front of the bus. It was unusual, no flack or smart-ass comment. This had to work, or I would never live down the moment.

"We good?" asked Tommy and Lee.

"Yes," I said, "Get ready, Jess!" I yelled. She started up the V.W. bus.

"Ready!" She yelled.

"LEE, Tommy… Push!" I yelled, then a second later, I yelled, "Jess, keep it in neutral and throttle it in reverse when I tell you!"

Jessie put her foot on the gas pedal with the bus in neutral. I pushed from the open side door watching the back tires while Lee and Tommy pushed the front of the van.

I yelled, "On three. One... Two... Three!

Jessie slammed it in reverse.

"Floor it!" We all yelled.

The tires spun, and got on the mats, launching the bus backward. When the bus finally got off the sand and onto the road, it shot off out of control. Jessie backed over a bunch of small boulders. The bus bounced all over, gliding over the rocks that hit the undercarriage. Jessie managed to clear the rocks and get the bus back onto a parking area near the road.

***

The sun was already setting, and we decided to stay one more night. Plus, Tommy and I both felt Jessie and Lee needed a little more time to cool off before we got back on the road.

Tommy took the time to teach me how to wax my surfboard better. He felt that was one of many reasons I was having a hard time getting up.

He said, "This is by far the single-most-important skill in surfing. Always remember, before tricks comes grip. May sound simple, but it's way important."

He went on to explain how hard wax was for the base and soft wax was for the top cause it's stickier that way. He seemed so thrilled that I even cared, and it was, by all means, an excellent way to pass the time without having to deal with Lee and Jessie's drama.

He went on to explain, "A base coat keeps the topcoat from rubbing off. Those dudes that go for that single-swipe-crap end up with wax-free areas on their deck after a few waves and end up doing cartwheels off the board."

Boy, I knew what that was like. I had only been using the soft wax. On examining my surfboard we found lots of spots were the wax had rubbed off. It was just like most things in life a well-disciplined or hard foundation was needed first. Tommy handed me the hard wax, and I rubbed it up and down my surfboard. He gently corrected my hand so I was holding the bar at a 45-degree angle.

I made about a dozen thick lines down the deck. Tommy watched me close, making sure I didn't miss anything. It was like having a big brother. It is funny, whenever I would say I wished I had a big brother or sister to anyone I knew who had siblings they would look at me like I was crazy. They'd say they wished they could be the only child like me. If they had spent as many quite afternoons alone in a home by themselves as I did, I'm sure they'd change their mind.

I finished the first coat and said, "How's that?"

"Nice," Tommy said. He handed me the soft wax and said, "Now, rub it in small circles."

I did what he said, but the wax was getting bumpy, and I wasn't sure I was doing it right.

"See those beads forming?" He asked. I sighed. He continued, "That's perfect!"

I felt good, that was until I looked down the shoreline. About a quarter mile down, Lee was tossing rocks into the ocean by himself. And a quarter mile in the opposite direction, Jessie sat reading by herself. I felt responsible. Although finding out about Jessie was bound to happen someday, why did it have to be now.

Tommy put some wood into the fire pit and lit it. The sun fell behind the ocean, but it was still pretty bright outside. Tommy and I sat there for a while, not saying anything.

I have an obsession with puzzles like both my parents. On the first Friday of every month, one of them would put out a 5000-piece jigsaw puzzle. By Sunday morning, it was always finished. It was one of those family traditions I loved. It was something that brought us closer as a family. I looked at Jessie sitting alone and felt like my love for puzzles wasn't bringing my friends closer together. It was tearing us all apart.

Tommy looked over at where Lee was and then at Jessie; and said, "This blows."

"Sorry," I said.

"Not your fault," he said, "It's just people."

"I don't see what the big deal is," I said.

"My mom and dad fight all the time, but that isn't as bad as the silence." He said. "I came out here to get as far away from that crap as I possibly could. Dude, this shit just keeps coming after me."

"What do we do?" I asked.

"Stay out of it and hope like hell they don't ask us to take sides." Tommy slid into his sleeping bags near the campfire. The stars brightened as the leftover sunlight faded. Lee and Jessie were no longer visible from where Tommy and I were. I wondered how people so close, could stay so mad at each other. I gazed over at Tommy and saw him trying to hide his tears. I gave silent thanks that my mom and dad, even though not around much, still loved each other like they did.

Chapter 11

Are there really Thirteen Ways of Looking at a Blackbird?

Tommy and I walked up to the shoreline together. The tide was up, but Lee and Jessie weren't. The bus was still there, but neither of them was anywhere we could see. It was so weird. So was the presence of all the crows. I never knew blackbirds would congregate at the beach. I was one of those kids that enjoyed reading the Encyclopedia Britannica. It was something that would take my mind off the boredom of being alone.

I had a new wax job and new confidence in having my first positive outcome with nature. The reason we had all the camping gear is that my parents thought it would be good for me to do the boy scout thing. And they were right, I flew through the merit badges, knots, sewing, memorizing manuals, I killed it. Until our first outing. What a disaster, poison oak, a broken leg, and we found out I was allergic to bees. Maybe I'm just allergic to nature in general.

Tommy glanced over at me and smiled. Now, if there was someone who had a handle on nature, it was him. Until yesterday, I only saw Tommy as a dumb jock that loved to surf more than breathe. And as usual, I was wrong, as I often am when it comes to understanding people. He had such kindness and patience. Qualities I could definitely stand to improve on in myself, as I hated anything, I couldn't get perfect the first time I did it.

"You got this, bro." Tommy said. He had waited at the shore's edge with me and called me his bro. This was a first on both accounts. I was moving up in the world, I had graduated from dude to bro. May sound trivial, but it really did make me feel part of the group, still kind of does.

We walked into the water together until it was waist high, then we hopped onto our surfboards. By now, Tommy would already be out taming the waves, but instead, this time, he hung with me.

"OK, we got to get beyond the waves before we can surf 'em." He sat upon his board and pointed, "Watch the waves."

"What am I looking for?" I asked.

"There are two types of waves you duck dive," Tommy said.

"Duck dive?" I asked.

He smiled and said, "It's the best way to save your juice while ducking under a wave with your surfboard. You'll either do it through a wave's whitewash or one that's not broken yet. Whitewash is the hardest. It's impossible to duck dive a powerful whitewater wave without speed. Think attack mode, don't hesitate, go straight into the wave, with loads of speed. Just before you get to the wave push the nose of your board down as hard as you can, kick one foot up in the air to help throw your weight down. Hang onto your board and pop out on the other side."

He made it sound so easy. Tommy nudged me, "Let's go after this next set."

My heart pounded. Although the waves did intimidate me, I was more worried about letting Tommy down.

"OK bro, let's do this," Tommy said. We paddled out together. "Faster! Go after it!" He yelled at me. I paddled as hard as I could. We got to about six feet in front of the wave when Tommy yelled, "Now!"

I shoved the tip of my board down as hard as I could. I could feel the force of the wave pushing on it, I hung on tight, then felt another force shove me from behind. I popped out of the water on the other side of the wave.

"Nice, bro." Tommy said.

I was ecstatic, I did it. I really did it! I had a whole new attitude. I was ready to go after a wave.

"Just focus on three things right now when you go for a wave, paddle to match its speed, look over your shoulder, when you feel the push pop up, got it?" Tommy asked.

"Got it," I said.

"Cool, watch me, then go for it." Tommy said.

He looked out over the water and spotted the swell he wanted like an eagle eyeing its prey. In seconds Tommy was lined up, and in front of the wave, he looked over his shoulder, and as the wave formed, he popped up on his board. It wasn't long before he disappeared into the tube.

I saw the swell I wanted and said to myself, "Come on, Ben, you got this." Moving my hands as fast as I could I propelled myself into the path of the wave. The wave formed as it pushed the back of the surfboard. I went to pop up and in the middle of popping up I thought crap, I forgot to look over my shoulder. My feet hit the deck of the surfboard and didn't slip off. I looked back, and the wave hit me in the head. I flew off the board headfirst. The wave slammed my head under the water and into the board, everything went black.

Weightless, it was weightlessness I felt first in the blackness. The sound was gone, just black weightlessness. I couldn't feel anything, not the cold, not my arms or legs, no pain, nothing. I couldn't even open my eyes though I wanted to. The first thing that seemed to work again was my hearing, but that was muffled and echoey. Lee's voice was the first voice I heard, and it felt like my body was being pulled through dark clouds.

"Ben!" Lee's voice echoed.

I felt a spinning sensation, and everything got brighter. But my eyelids still weren't working. I couldn't open them.

"Ben! Come on dude! Wake up!" Lee's voice echoed. "NO, no no no, come on, buddy, wake up! This can't be happening; it can't be happening!"

Tommy's voice then echoed in my head, "DUDE! What do we do? What the hell do we do!"

Jessie's echoes blended with the others, "Oh my God!"

"Ben!" Lee said. I tried to answer them, but nothing worked, it was like being trapped in some kind of dark box. I was glad, though, to hear Lee's and Jessie's voice in such close proximity to each other.

I finally got my eyelids to open, and all my senses came back all at once like a ton of bricks falling on me. Jessie's face was right above mine. She pinched my nose with her fingers and then kissed me. It was the first time I had a girl's lips on mine, and it felt awesome. I should have responded sooner but I was enjoying it too much. That was till she blew air into me, that didn't feel so good. Less than a second later, it felt like my ribs were being crushed into my spine. I could clearly hear them all pop, and I thought for sure, at least one of them broke. I never did have a high tolerance to pain, so I squealed and cried out.

Tommy said to Jessie, "Sick."

"Big-time, nice Jess," Lee said. He smiled at me and helped me to my feet, saying, "Thought we lost our D'Artagnan there for a minute."

***

Sitting in the back of the bus, I held an ice pack on my head and one on my ribs. I watched Tommy, Lee, and Jessie laughing and joking with each other. For the moment, bitterness and anger had been eliminated from our group. Lee shocked me when he referred to me as D'Artagnan. Tommy, of course, had no clue what Lee was referring to at the moment, but I knew exactly who he was. He was the fourth musketeer. Not only that, but he was also the central character of Dumas' novel.

You could say anything you want about Lee, but if there was anyone who would be willing to put their life in jeopardy to save someone else, it was him. Even with his flaws, there was no one I've ever known capable of being a better friend. And now I knew, I was much more than a third wheel, I was one of the musketeers.

I never had the heart to tell Jessie that I had a concussion, not a heart attack. She kind of forgot to check for a pulse. I kind of enjoyed her mouth on mine. Even though I had a splitting headache and was unable to breathe, it was all worth it to see everyone getting along again.

The V.W. bus sputtered, jerked, and stalled out. The bus slowed as it coasted to stop. Jessie steered it to the side of the road before it completely stopped moving.

"Gas?" Tommy asked.

Jessie looked at the last mileage she recorded and then the odometer. "No, we have over half," she said. Jessie looked in the rearview mirror and sighed. "Crap!"

I looked out the back window, and there was a long small trail of what appeared to be gas.

Jessie hit the steering wheel and threw open the door. She got out and stormed to the back of the bus. Tommy hopped out from the passenger side, over her seat, following close behind. Lee shook his head and laughed.

"What's so funny?" I asked. I didn't find the situation funny at all. We were on a road in the middle of Mexico, with no gas.

"He's got it bad." He said.

"What?" I asked.

"He's tripping on Jess."

"Wait… Tommy likes Jess? I asked Lee, nodded, "Like, likes Jess? Like more than just friends?"

Lee laughed even harder, "He's whipped. Ever since Jess saved you, he can't take his eyes off her."

I watched out the back as Jessie checked the engine. Lee was right. And Tommy's ogling was making her totally uncomfortable. She leaned into the engine compartment, and when she came back out, she had grease on her face.

"You know, I never noticed before, but you're like kind of hot." Tommy said. Lee and I both giggled. Jessie saw her reflection in the window of the back of the bus. I guess seeing the grease on her face pissed her off because she looked at Tommy and said, "You're such a dick!" Then she wiped some of the grease off her face and rubbed it on his. The funniest part was that she walked away pissed, and Tommy looked like he had just been kissed by a prom queen.

Jessie hopped back into the front of the bus and hit the roof with her hand, yelling, "Shit!"

Lee said to her, "Good news, I take it?"

"We have a torn hose," Jessie said.

"Anyway to fix it?" I asked.

She answered, "Not that I know of."

"Got any spare hoses?" Tommy asked.

Laughing, Lee said, "No. That's her problem. She doesn't have a hose."

Jessie flipped Lee off, and he laughed harder. They exchange looks. She looked pissed off at first but busted up laughing with Lee.

"There was a general store we passed not too long ago." Lee said.

"Yeah! That gas station one," Tommy said.

"We'll need some gas cans, gas, and some tape," Jessie said.

"I could go with Jess and get—" Tommy began.

"Yeah, I bet," Lee said, cutting him off. "I think we will all need to go. Gas cans aren't light."

I grabbed my backpack and emptied my duffle. That way, if we got there and they didn't have bags, we'd have something to carry stuff back in. I put on some extra sunscreen.

"Ben! Come on, dude, we'd be on our way back by now." Lee said.

I passed the cooler and grabbed some sodas for everyone too.

Chapter 12

How did we find ourselves in the disillusionment of Ten O'Clock?

We all walked down the road in the direction of the Corner Store we passed a while back on the highway we were on. I got a root beer for Jessie, a Mountain Dew for Lee, and a Pepsi for Tommy. It wasn't but a few minutes of walking in the sun before Tommy said, "I'm parched."

"Me too," Jessie said.

"What do you want to bet D'Artagnan here got our backs," Lee said.

I smiled and handed them all their drinks. I, of course, had a Mountain Dew. I didn't like them as much as sprites, but at that time, I was a little bit of a Lee-wanna-be.

"So who's Porthos?" I asked.

"That would be Lee, and I'm Athos," Jessie said.

"I thought I was Athos," Tommy said.

"Aramis," Lee corrected.

"Oh yeah, they sound the same," Tommy said.

"You should try reading the book someday, bro." Lee said to him. I had a hard time picturing Lee sitting down and reading a book. But there were times when he would say things that made me think he was actually well-read.

"Why I'll just watch the movie. Zorro and the Three Musketeers was bad dude."

"Bad as in good or bad as in bad?" I asked.

"It was righteous, totally excellent bro." Tommy explained.

I had never heard of the movie, but Tommy knew his films. And if he said it was a movie, then it was. Whether it was good or not, that was something debatable.

Have you ever walked on a dirt road and got a pebble in your shoe? And when you stopped to take it out, it ended up right back where it was? It was making me crazy. I'm not one for deserts at all, I generally like lush green landscapes. The browns were plentiful in this place. Not one blade of grass was green. Yet the golden tones mixed with this desert landscape in its own way to create a unique beauty. The road blended with the horizon ahead in waves.

I was enjoying the silent walking, other than that damn pebble.

Tommy turned to Lee and said, "Now that the truth is out on Jess, why don't you tell us what happened?"

"When?" I asked.

Lee pulled the last cigarette out of a pack, sighed, crumpled it up, and tossed it.

"Hey!" I yelled, he looked at me as I picked it up, "Give a hoot." Tommy and Jessie joined in, but with a lot more sarcasm. And said, "And don't pollute." Then they all laughed at me. I didn't care, I'd still yell at someone today for doing that. Littering is and has always been a hot button for me. If everyone just picked up after themselves, the world would be a hell of a lot better place.

"You've never said what you did to end up in juvie," Jessie said.

"He didn't do anything. He was framed or something," I said.

Lee lit his cigarette and smiled at me. That smile told me everything I needed to know. It was him saying I was right. After playing poker with him, I knew his look for a bluff, and that smile was no bluff.

"Dude, whatever," Tommy said to me. He redirected his attention to Lee and said, "Come on, just spill it."

Lee just laughed at him. I think mainly because Lee knew that the truth wasn't near as entertaining as a mystery. And I think at that time Lee thrived on being a mystery to people.

The small Corner Store, as it said in Spanish, came into view we were almost there. Two gas pumps stood evenly spaced in front of the store. They had nearly as much rust around them as the awning that covered them. The dirt was layered over the white paint on the building creating tons of patterns in it. It was hard to tell if anyone had ever actually cleaned the place.

"Did you kill someone?" Jessie asked.

Sarcastically Lee said, "Yeah, I went on a killing spree."

"Did you wank off in front of the po-po?" Tommy asked.

We all laughed, Tommy always went there, and it was only a matter of time before he got even more raunchy.

"Did you set a house on fire?" Jessie asked.

Lee shook his head, no.

"Dude, did you like do a cop's daughter?" Tommy asked.

"Do you ever think about anything else?" Jessie asked Tommy.

"No." Tommy answered and then said, "Dude! I know! He got caught banging the neighbor's dog." And there it was, right on time, Tommy taking it too far.

"Gross!" I said.

"Grody!" said Jessie.

With a deadpan look on his face, Lee said, "Wow, Tommy, you finally figured it out."

"Really?!" Jessie asked.

Lee walked up to the entrance of the Corner Store, opened the door, and said, "No. Now drop it already." He held the door open for all of us to go in. It was surprisingly a lot cleaner on the inside and much more significant than it looked on the outside. Guess that's why you can't judge a book by its cover.

The back two walls were lined with a refrigerated section. It didn't look all that different than a Stop-and-Go from back home. My parents didn't like me going to them even though they had better Slurpees than 7-Eleven. They called them "Stop and robs." I think mainly because they had a few too many of their patrons as patients.

"Check out these fireworks!" Tommy announced.

He waved me over to where he was. There were two sections of shelves dedicated to fireworks, all the standard ones like fountains, sparklers, and flowers. Then there was a whole section of fireworks I had never seen before. They were these big old boxes with fuses on them. Tommy pointed to the one that said the devil's revenge in Spanish.

"What do you think?" He asked.

"About what?" I asked.

"Getting some." Tommy said.

Fireworks were another bone of contention with my parents. We didn't spend many Fourth of Julys together. They got called into the hospital every year with a line of people who did something stupid or had one of those things misfire and take out a vital chunk of their flesh. They said Roman Candles were one of the worst.

"How about some sparklers?" I said.

"And?" he asked.

"Flowers and fountains, but none of those." I said, pointing to the Roman Candles.

"Cool," he said and pointed to the row of boxes that said devil's revenge in Spanish, "You gotta let me score some of these too."

"OK. You can grab one." I said.

"Sweet!" Tommy said.

Lee yelled from across the store, "Hey, I found some tape."

Jessie yelled back, "Let me look."

I went over to where Lee was as Tommy grabbed a bunch of fireworks. I saw him grab a Roman Candle and yelled at him, "Put it back!" he nodded and put it back. I thought, is this how my parents feel all the time? If so, I decided right then, and there, I would never have kids.

Jessie looked at the two different types of duct tape they had and grabbed one. Lee grabbed some cheese whiz and crackers that were on the shelf next to where the tape was.

"Might as well grab one more," I said.

"Cool," Lee said.

He walked off and I said to Jessie, "I meant for you to grab one more."

"One of each?" She asked.

"Which one do you think will work?" I asked.

"Not sure," Jessie said.

"Then get two of each," I said. I figured better safe than sorry. We finally got all our crap up to the checkout desk. I looked at all the stuff and thought, how the hell are we going to walk back to the bus with it? I looked around and noticed a red wagon next to some 5-gallon gas cans. I left the counter and grabbed them. We all almost completely forgot about needing to get gas.

I left my dad's credit card on the counter. I took the wagon and gas cans out to the pumping station and filled them up as the others got some drinks. It didn't take too long to fill up the first one. I picked it up, and it was pretty heavy. I got wiser on the second one and set it on the wagon before I started filling it up. Lee came out holding my duffle bag that was now stuffed so full there was no way to zip it up. He handed me the credit card.

"All good," Lee said.

"Don't I need to sign for it?"

"Nope, I got it for you," Tommy said.

And with that, we started our trek back to the bus.

***

The wagon was a great idea but was still a bear to pull. We got so much stuff and I did read the gas cans wrong. They were ten gallons, not five. Thankfully we all took turns pulling. Tommy started in on how pissed he was that his mom was moving.

"So why is your mom moving back to China, or was that just an exaggeration?" I asked.

"Nope, not an exaggeration," Tommy said, "she's really going there. Sucks too. She's way nicer than dad-"

Jessie interrupted, "His mom doesn't beat him if he misses a pass in practice."

"True dat." Lee said.

"Seriously, your dad beats you if you miss a pass?"

Tommy nodded.

"Why don't you quit?" I asked.

"One, I like football almost as much as I like surfing. And two, he'd kick my ass even harder if I quit."

"Typical, I had an Asian guy in juvie whose dad kicked the shit out of him if he got A minuses in school."

"You guys know, Quan?" Jessie asked we all nodded, "Yeah, well, her dad's the same way."

"Is that like a Chinese thing then?" I asked Tommy.

"No, Nakamura is Japanese." Tommy said.

"His dad's a Nip." Lee said.

"OK, Pedro," Tommy said and continued, "At least I know who my dad is."

Lee flipped off Tommy and he, along with Jessie, laughed.

"Pedro?" I asked.

"Yeah," Jessie said, "It's his *real* name."

"Really?" I asked.

"Totally, he has a thing for the Bionic Man." Tommy said.

"Oh! I love that show," I said, "So why did you pick a different name?" I asked Lee.

"Because I hate the son of a bitch, I'm named after." Lee said. We were all quiet again and walked in silence for a few minutes. I still didn't know if Tommy was going to China with his mom, made sense, but he said before we left on our trip, he was going to Chicago. It was driving me nuts I had to know.

"So, are you going to China?" I asked.

"Hell, no!" Tommy said.

"But you said—"

"My dad may be a dick, but I ain't going to a bunch of rice paddies in the middle of nowhere. Just sucks is all."

"Yeah, it does," Jessie said.

How would I choose? I love both my parents. Dad's harder on the discipline but lets me do more cool things. Mom totally allows me to get away with things, but if it was up to her, I'm sure I'd still be in a playpen. What if their views of religion split them up? How would I choose one way to worship God over another, when in truth, they are accomplishing the same thing?

Then there was Lee. Did he really hate his dad because he never knew him? Or was it because he wasn't there to protect him from people like Vern? Lee and the bionic man. I mean, who didn't like Lee Majors, he was cool. But what was the attraction? I didn't want another Jessie incident on this trip. I figured it'd be best to let this puzzle go.

Chapter 13

What does it mean when The Wind Shifts?

We got back to the bus, and well, it wasn't quite how we left it.

"What the hell!" Lee yelled.

"Someone kyped our stuff!" Tommy said.

"This isn't happening." Jessie said.

I was so relieved that I had my backpack. If someone would have taken my journal I would have been crushed. We climbed into the bus, and it was cleaned out, no cooler, no sleeping bags, no surfboards. Whoever did this even took the hubcaps off the car. Probably lucky we got back when we did, or I'm sure a lot more parts would have been missing.

After we got past the initial shock, we quickly came to the realization that we still had to fix the bus or we would be stuck there for the night.

Jessie wrapped tape all over the hoses and said, "I think that's the last one. Try again."

Lee poured in the gas as Tommy and I looked for leaks. I got the job of being under the bus because I was the smallest. Understandable, but it still sucked. I had a deathly fear of spiders and scorpions or any other thing that crawled unnaturally. And when you're in a shaded place where it's hot and arid, all kinds of things crawl all over you.

I didn't know what was worse, the critters crawling on me or the crap on the underside of the V.W. bus that would fall in my face. I watched to see if anything dripped. I spotted a section of the undercarriage a few feet away from me that looked dented, and the caked-on grease sludge that made up the underside of the bus was scraped off. I scooted across the gravelly dirt on my back over to it to inspect it.

A piece of glass snagged my shirt as I wiggled over under the spot. It sliced me and my shirt, and it stung bad. My back sting wasn't what had me pissed as much as this was my favorite shirt! Why does shit always happen to your favorite clothes? They're the ones you spill cherry juice on, get a grass stain on, or grease up and slice open with a stupid ass piece of glass that if someone had just thrown it away, my shirt would have still been savable!

A gas drop fell right onto my eye, fueling my anger. "Stop! Found another one," I yelled. Jessie popped her head down.

"Need any help getting to it?" she asked.

I probably could have done it by myself, but I was sick of being down here all alone. "I wouldn't mind a hand," I said. Jessie got down to crawl under the bus with me. "Careful, there's glass down here." I warned, she thanked me and cautiously made her way over to me.

"It's right here," I said, pointing to the leak.

"Let's hope this is the last one," she said.

She pulled off some duct tape, tore it off, and maneuvered her hand around her body. She tried to make sure the tape didn't make contact with the ground, the greasy undercarriage, or itself. She got it up to the hose and the duct tape folded in on itself. "Shit!" she said. And tossed the tape. I looked at her like I did Lee when he threw his wrapper. She said, "Don't you dare! I'll pick it up later." I distinctly remembered that face, it was one my mom gave my dad often, and now I knew first-hand the power it contained.

"Want me to put my hand next to the hose to help grab the tape?" I asked.

"Yeah." She said and pulled off another piece of duct tape. She pulled it across her body, and it snagged her shirt, she peeled it off and when it let loose it flung up and hit the greasy underside of the bus dropping grease on her face, some fell in her mouth. "Son of a bitch! You cock sucking piece of shit!" I tried not to laugh, tears welled in my eyes, and I clamped down my lips as hard as I could.

I'm sure there must be something wrong in enjoying someone else's misery, but there I was finding humor in hers. Jessie pulled off another section of tape, I was able to reach the other end, and we were able to tightly wrap it around the leaky spot. She looked at me and gave a sigh of relief.

"Third time's the charm, right? I asked.

She glared at me and said, "Thank you for not laughing, or I would have had to kill you." She turned her head away from me and yelled, "OK, try again."

Lee poured in more gas.

Jessie watched closely, and no gas dripped where we were, "I don't see anything leaking," she said.

"Me either," I said.

"Dude looks good from here too," Tommy said.

***

Back at the Corner Store. Jessie pumped the gas as we raided the store for a few more supplies. At this point, we were just getting enough stuff to get us back home. We agreed to let Tommy shoot off all the fireworks before we crossed back over the border. Another problem we hadn't considered. Without June and April, how were we going to get home? I did have my passport, and hopefully, that would be enough.

We walked out of the Corner Store. Jessie put the pump back, and this local kid who looked about eight randomly walked up. His brown pants were about two sizes too small. The white ribbed t-shirt appeared well worn and clean. He passed us all up and went straight for Lee.

In Spanish, the kid said to Lee, "Hey, I know who took your stuff."

"No, speak Mexican," Lee said.

"I thought you were Mexican," Jessie said.

"I am," Lee said.

"You don't know how to speak Spanish?" Tommy asked. Leave it to Tommy to reinforce stereotypes. Then again, how can you live in Southern California and not know at least a little Spanish? My parents spoke it fluently. I will say the dialect the kid was using was hard to understand. I was pretty sure he was trying to tell us where our stuff was. He could have been asking for our stuff too.

"What do you think! Just cause I'm Mexican, I can automatically speak it? Do you speak Chinese?" Lee asked.

"No, but--"

"The stuff that was stolen from the bus over there?" I asked in Spanish

The local kid in Spanish said, "Yes. Trejo's guys took it."

"Who's that?" I asked in Spanish.

He replied in Spanish, "I'll show you. Ten pesos."

"What's he saying?" Jessie asked.

I told her, "Says he knows where our stuff is."

"What are we waiting for?" Lee asked.

"Yeah!" Tommy added.

"He says he needs ten pesos," I answered.

"How about ten knuckles, think he'd understand that?" Lee asked.

Tommy looked at Lee and said, "Chill, our stuff man."

"Do we have any pesos?" Jessie asked.

We dug through our pockets. Tommy pulled out a pack of gum and opened it spitting out the gum he was chewing. The local kid pointed at his gum. and in Spanish said, "That will work."

"Now what?" Lee asked.

"He said he'd take Tommy's gum," I answered.

"What!?" Tommy asked.

Lee snatched the gum out of Tommy's hand before he could pull a piece for himself and handed it to the kid.

"What the hell!" Tommy said annoyed.

The kid said, "Follow me," to us in Spanish. I told the others what he wanted, and we followed him to a beat-up old truck with an older man at the wheel. This was a pretty rough looking area, but Lee hopped into the truck with the old man and the kid without even debating it. The rest of us got in the bus and followed them

Chapter 14

Can we see Ghosts as Cocoons?

We pulled in front of a cluster of shack-like houses. It was something you'd see in a bad western. Lee got out of the rusted red pick-up truck. The kid and older man stayed in the truck and fought over something; I couldn't quite understand them. They were talking way too fast. The kid got out of the truck and stood next to it. We met up with Lee near the front of what looked to be the main house. I think a bewildered feeling overcame all of us. For once, I wasn't the only one who was scared shitless.

A giant scary-looking, muscular dude, walked out of the door and waved at us to come inside. No shirt, new-looking jeans, and black cowboy boots. I was making an educated guess that his name was Juan as it was tattooed across his chest. Along with a ton of other tattoos. We just stood there, silent.

"Come in," he said in Spanish, "Come in."

The local kid flipped out and got back in the truck with the older man. Before the door was shut, the truck tore off down the dirt road, leaving a cloud of dust. We looked at each other like let's get the hell out of here. Jessie looked back at the house. Juan kept motioning for us to come in.

Lee, Tommy, and I backed up slowly to the V.W. bus. Jessie looked at us and then looked at the guy at the door again. She had this look of determination and walked right past the scary behemoth of a man into the house. Now, what choice did we have? We had to go in.

We walked in behind Jessie. The room was large enough to comfortably fit several couches and at least twenty or so terrifying guys with guns, lots of guns. There was a haze of skunky smelling smoke moving through the room.

A Mexican Mafia type, very rough looking, sat in the middle of a bunch of other Mexicans packed into the place. He had long dark hair pulled back into a ponytail. Tough leathery skin with a full mustache that reached his strong jawline. I was drawn to the tattoo that covered the bulk of his chest of a woman wearing a sombrero and the falling dove on his right bicep. His eyes commanded respect from all the others in the room. He had to be the guy the kid was talking about, he was Trejo.

All these tatted-up dudes who looked like they just got out of prison stared at us, waiting for a command from their boss. Jessie walked into the middle of them. Trejo made eye contact with her.

Trejo stood up. Jessie glared at him, and he glared back at her. They looked as though they were having a silent gun slinging contest. It wasn't long before Trejo smiled.

Trejo asked, "You here for something?"

"Yes. Our surfboards, our clothes, and my rims! We want them back." Jessie answered him.

All the Mexicans in the room brandished their weapons. I thought to myself, well, that's it. I'm not going to have to worry about my parents killing me, because I was going to die here. Trejo put up his hand as a signal to calm down. He said,

"You got some big cojones." He looked pissed. I kept thinking, let's just go. Let's just go home and chalk this whole trip to a horrible idea.

"No!" Jessie said.

"No?" Trejo asked.

"I've got no cojones, I'm PMSing!" She said.

All the Mexicans in the room laughed. I was thinking, they're laughing, their guns are down, let's get the hell out of here. April and June entered the room from a dark hallway.

April said to us, "Hey, guys." There was a new calmness in the room. Most of the guys that were gripping their pistols put them away. My heart was still racing, but it was back in my chest instead of in my throat.

June smiled at us then turned to Trejo and said, "Hey cuz, these are the kids that got us over the border."

"Get out!" Trejo said.

"No, they are," April said.

Trejo laughed and extended his hand to Jessie. She shook it. "Very well," he said, "You want your stuff back?"

We all nodded. Trejo looked at an old white man with a long grey beard sitting next to him. He looked like a skinny version of Santa Clause. The red t-shit would have completed the look except for the fact it said eat shit and die. That was where the Santa imagery kind of got lost on me. The Santa man pulled out a deck of cards. He said, "One card draw?"

Jessie looked back at Lee. Lee grinned and said, "You're on." Lee pointed to me and said, "And he deals."

I about crapped myself and shook my head no. Trejo looked at me, smiled and said, "Let's do this."

***

We were ushered through a spiderweb of darkened hallways to a room with a shop light dangling over a steel table. Juan pulled out an old wooden chair for me to sit on. It was surprisingly comfortable. Trejo sat down across from me. He was no different than the bunch of the sharks Uncle John used me to play against.

He was studying me right away. Here's the thing, I had to be a dumb, scared kid. If I wasn't, he'd know something was up. Not too hard to do at this point, I was scared. I also couldn't study him; he'd see it and know something was up. I sat at a table and stared at the cards I didn't ever want to make eye contact; he was watching me like my uncle watched people. And very little if anything got by Uncle John. I wished he were here instead of me right now. I looked behind me. Lee, Tommy, and Jessie stood behind me totally overconfident. Crap, if they don't play it down a little, we're going to get so busted.

I felt like a scared rabbit in front of a hungry wolf. I picked up the cards and shuffled them. I let my hands shake instead of controlling them so my card handling would look a little less polished.

Trejo watched me and chuckled. This didn't make me feel all that sure about what I was about to try and pull off. Well, here goes nothing, I thought. I set the deck in front of Trejo to cut. He cut the deck dead-center. I was right on where he'd cut it. Now the scary part. Seeing if I placed the cards in the right place.

He slid the deck back to me. I let out a long sigh. I still didn't make direct eye contact with him. I dealt one card to Trejo, and one to myself. I set the deck back down in the middle between us.

Trejo smiled, never taking his eyes off me, and flipped his card over, reveling a Jack of Hearts. I flipped over the King of Spades. Jessie, Tommy, and Lee smiled at each other.

"Nicely played kid," Trejo said. "But you cheated."

My face sunk, and Trejo pulled out a small colt cobra .38 special revolver. He flipped open the cylinder. He slid a bullet into each of the six spaces. Grinned at me, spun the cylinder, and with a whipping motion, slammed the cylinder back in place. There was now a loaded gun pointed right at me. He winked at me and set it next to the cards on the table. We all look terrified.

“Your crew gave you away. No poker faces,” Trejo said, "So if you're going to cheat for these guys, you better be able to back it up." He laughed and went on to say, "I like you, kids. Takes guts to do what you did." He looked at me and then to the gun and said, “Go on, take it."

***

We drove away from Trejo’s, and I sat there feeling ill as I stared out the window from the end of the bus. Trejo didn't give us everything he took, but we could care less at that point, we had survived. It was no place for a bunch of dumb kids like us to be in the first place.

I didn’t want his gun either, but as Uncle John always said, never kick a gift horse in the mouth. Having a loaded weapon around terrified me. I couldn’t just toss it. If some kid somewhere found it, I didn’t even want to think about it. Lee wanted it. I told him he could have it until we got back home, but once we’re home, it’s going to someone who can properly get rid of it.

I felt used, like last summer, and was more homesick than ever. I closed my eyes for what I thought was only a second when I felt something crawling on my nose. I smacked at my head and had a face full of whipped cream.

Lee, Tommy, and Jessie were laughing hysterically.

"Dude, we're here!" Tommy said.

"What?" I asked.

"We made it. You have to come see!" Jessie said.

"See what?" I asked.

"Mushrooms," Lee said.

***

I stayed in the shallows, trying to surf the whitewash. I didn't want to drink any more saltwater or get bashed in the head by my surfboard. I was content right where I was. I would have stayed on shore, but it was so hot that I wanted to cool off a little. And as soon as the heat was bearable, I was getting out of the water.

Tommy and Jessie went out pretty far and caught some very massive-looking waves. Lee paddled past me to join them.

I sat on my surfboard and watched Lee finally get up and ride a wave in. It was refreshing to see his excitement. He paddled back out and stopped by me.

"Come on!" He said.

"There're waves here," I said.

"It's ripping out there. Come on, you'll love it!"

"There could be big sharks out that deep," I said. It's one thing to go out a few yards or so into the ocean. It's quite another thing to go out a few hundred yards. Plus, I didn't swim all that well, and my last few experiences with waves hadn't built much confidence. Nope, I just wanted to stay right where I was until it cooled off.

I didn't see Tommy, but Jessie sailed into the tube of a wave. And Lee said,

"Live a little. Crash that bubble you hide in."

"I just--"

"Hey, it's your loss, man," he said.

A few feet away, a fin popped out of the water. I pointed and shouted, "Lee!"

Lee looked and said, "Oh, crap!"

Lee and I high tailed it out of the water. Tommy popped out of the water where we were, and bursts into laughter. He had a shark fin in his hands. Lee and I wanted to kill him.

Karma's a bitch though, because as Tommy was laughing at us, a dark shadow approached from a few yards behind Tommy, and a fin broke the surface. Lee, Jessie, and I pointed at it from the shore.

Jessie yelled, "Behind you!" I yelled, "Swim in!" and Lee yelled, "Get out of the water!"

We all motioned for Tommy to get into shore. When Tommy finally looked behind himself and saw the dark shadow in the water, he panicked and dropped the fin. It looked like he was actually walking on water as fast as he swam in.

He got to the shore, barely able to breathe and hunched over. When he stood up to take in a breath of air Lee smacked him in the back of the head.

"Ass!" Lee yelled at him.

"Sorry. Just was trying to show Ben there was nothing to worry about." Tommy said. I think at this point, his plan completely backfired. I'm sure the rotting flesh from the fin he was holding acted like a homing signal for what looked to be a gigantic shark.

"Where did you find that thing anyway?" Jessie asked Tommy.

"What thing?" Tommy asked

"The fin genius," Lee said.

"Oh! You guys gotta check this out," Tommy replied.

***

On the other side of some bluffs was a secluded beach. Tommy pointed to a dead, great white shark that was the size of a small truck. We all looked at it in awe.

Tommy said, "I was checking it out, and the fin just fell off."

"I've never seen anything this massive in person," I said. I bent over and pulled on one of the shark's teeth where the jaw was broken, and it came off.

"Cool, isn't it?" Tommy asked.

"Damn," Lee said, and Jessie added, "Way cool."

"Hard to believe these things are always out there with us in the water," I commented. In that second, we all had a moment of bewildered silence, as we admired the presence of the massive creature.

Chapter 15

What is it about Sunday Morning?

Tommy started the evening by setting off fireworks. It wasn't long before Lee and Jessie joined him. I was happy, just watching. Tommy and Lee eventually convinced me to set off a few as well. They took turns, running up to the fireworks, lighting them, and running back to the campfire.

They all enjoyed the show. Lee set the last one off and ran back. We all watched while sitting by the fire. A loud thud and a professional-looking firework lit the sky. We marveled, watching it until the last of it faded.

Tommy looked at me and said, "That rocked!"

"Second that," Jessie said.

I nodded, but my heart wasn't in it, and I'm sure it showed.

Lee asked, "What's up?"

"I, well, I just want to go home," I said.

"What!?" Jessie asked.

"You're such a jokester," Tommy said.

I was in no way joking. They might have been having the time of their lives, but I wasn't. The guilt had been growing and was winning. I kept thinking about what the hell I was going to tell my parents. I imagined the look on their faces when they got back. Thirteen years of building trust right out the window. The sad thing was, I wasn't having a good time. Why did I need to come all this way to figure out that I was better off to be alone and be true to myself than to become something I wasn't to make someone else happy, just so they would like me?

"No, really. I want to go home," I said.

"What! Why?" Lee asked.

"He misses his mommy," Tommy said.

"Come on, we just got here!" Jessie explained, "And you haven't even gotten up yet! Just give it a few days--"

"Friggin mama's boy!" Tommy yelled.

I was about to lose it but kept my cool. I said, "I don't want to. I want to go home. We said one week, that was it, and nothing about going to Mexico!"

"Don't puss out on us! I thought we were friends," Jessie said.

"What a buzzkill," Lee added, "Have some respect for yourself for once."

I'm sure my face was turning red as my anger continued to boil inside me. Then Tommy said, "I think he's gonna cry." That was the straw that broke the camel's back. I yelled at him, "You're an asshole!"

"No wonder you don't have any friends," Lee said.

I had no idea what utter betrayal felt like until that moment and completely lost it. I yelled at them, "All any of you ever wanted to do, is use me!"

I wanted to say more, but I couldn't get out the words. I instead stormed off. Tommy got up like he was going to give me a piece of his mind. But Lee pulled him back down. I could still hear them, as they weren't exactly quiet.

"What a little punk!" Tommy yelled.

“Wait...is he all that wrong?" Lee asked, "Haven't we though?" Lee got up and chased after me.

I made it up onto a bluff overlooking the fire. I sat there facing the ocean, as Lee approached. "Sorry," He said, "I didn't mean what I said. I should have never said those things. I'm sorry, man."

I just sat staring off into the ocean.

"Hope we're still cool," he said.

"Everyone thinks I'm a wuss," I said.

Lee looked at me and said, "I don't."

"Yeah, sure.” I said.

"No," he said, "I mean it. You're a good friend, you're real."

"Doesn't change the fact that I'm still a wuss," I said. I looked at him and continued, "You know it's funny, the person you see in the mirror isn't what everyone else sees. And when you finally see how they see you, you realize you've been living in a dream and what's real, really sucks." I took in a deep breath and said, "Nobody said anything that wasn't true. It just sucks to know that's what's real. Plus, I love my mom and dad, I know you all may not understand that, but I feel terrible right now. I am a wuss."

"I'm afraid of a lot of things. I was even afraid of José Lòpez," Lee said.

"Yeah, but you don't let your fear rule your life," I said.

"Yeah, I do," he said. "I just do the opposite of you, even when I know it's ‘terrible.’ I'm always doing stupid things just to prove I'm not afraid. Like what I said back there." Lee sighed and asked, "So, I need to know, are we cool?"

"Sure," I said. "You were really afraid of José Lòpez?"

Lee smiled and said, "Till I hit him... a little, but he was just a bully." I let out a sad sigh and Lee said, "Hey! We all need help fighting bullies sometimes."

"You're just saying this to make me feel better," I said.

"Hey, here's the real deal, I cried every night when I first got to juvie... got the shit kicked out of me every single day. It wasn't till this chaplain dude talked to the guards for me that things got better."

Lee smiled, "He gave me this poetry book. It was mad thick, written by this old white dude named Stevens, but it helped me. It helped get through the darkness I felt inside by showing me there was beauty in the winter, in the bleakness, and even in death. My favorite was this poem, Sunday Morning. I read it over and over again. He wrote this powerful line, '*Death is the mother of Beauty; hence from her, alone, shall come fulfillment to our dreams and our desires.'* The poem helped me feel like someday I would have a chance at a regular life."

Lee took a moment and then confessed, "But when I got out, nobody ever saw me as anything but the bad kid. So, I shut them out. I'm always afraid to let anyone know what's really on the inside, until, till that day, when I saw you, and you needed my help. But... you're like the first person since to really give a shit, and I like, messed it up. The one person who saw the best in me, I screwed over." I looked at him, and Lee had tears streaming down his cheeks.

"Why can't you trust anyone?" I asked.

"Guess cause of my mom," he said.

"What did she do?" I asked.

Lee nodded his head and wiped his eyes, "This is just between you and me, cool?" I nodded my head, and he continued, "Cops came to our house. At the time, I had no clue why. My mom didn't have time to hide her stash, so she stuffed it in my backpack. I was at the dinner table and didn't know. When the dogs found my bag, the cop asked if it was mine. I said it was. Then he asked if the drugs in it were mine."

He went on, "I said no, but my mom said she had suspected that I had been doing them for a while. I looked at her like, how could you, but she never looked back at me." Lee's voice wavered as he tried not to cry. "They put cuffs on me and put me in the back of the squad car. My own mom just watched as they took me away."

I put my arms around Lee, he collapsed into me and wept. Crying, he said, "She just watched. I mean, she just watched. She never even came to visit me, she just let them take me away." I just held him. I could feel his tears soak through my sweatshirt. It took him a while to composes himself, and then he said, "I am afraid... I'm afraid to go home, that's why I got so mad. I don't want to go home."

"Then don't," I said. "When we get back, you can move in with me."

"What about your mom and dad?" He asked.

I knew Mom and Dad already said he was welcome, but I thought I'd try to add a little levity and said, "They're never home anyway, probably wouldn't even know you were there."

He laughed and said his standard, "Dude."

"I already told them about you," I said, "And they said you can stay any time you want."

"I got to go back to Vern's one more time."

"Why?" I asked.

"The only thing that's good about me is there." I looked at him like what? He went on to say, "A gold medal... When I was like little, my grandpa gave me this medal he won when he was in the Olympics. I have to find it before my mom, so she doesn't sell it."

"Then, let's get it back!" I said.

Lee smiled, stood up, and looked over at the others still sitting by the fire.

He said, "You coming back?"

I looked at the ocean and said, "No, not tonight."

"OK," he said, "I'll go get my bag and be right back."

"No, I'll be fine," I said. "I want to have some time to myself."

"But we're cool, right?" Lee asked.

I nodded, and he left. I watched Lee walk away to the campfire with Jessie and Tommy. I thought I had a crappy life. I used to wish I could be Tommy, the most popular kid in school, or Jessie, one of the best athletes in the county, or even Lee, who was a legendary badass. They all seemed so cool.

Sitting there, I realized I had it pretty damn good. I thought about my mom and dad. I knew there'd be hell to pay, but I needed to tell them the truth. I think I finally figured out that doing the brave thing, was doing the right thing. I thought about the bullies in my life. That sharks out there, José Lòpez, feeling lonely and being afraid.

I was brought back to something I heard once in Sunday School... God only works when you trust him. Supposedly, Christians have nothing to fear, so why was I always afraid? I never heard God, but then again, I kind of treated him like a Genie that never granted my wishes. Maybe it was time to really test what I believed.

I watched the sunlight separate the ocean from the sky. I had made up my mind. I wasn't leaving until I caught a wave or was shark food. I told God I was sorry for the way I treated him, asked for forgiveness, and to join me for a walk on the water.

I got up, grabbed my surfboard, and walked to the water's edge. I looked out over the ocean. The sun was cresting over the horizon. The waves hit my feet, and I took in a deep breath. I walked into the water until it was too deep to walk and hopped on the board.

I paddled after a wave. It pushed hard, I popped up. When my right foot hit the board, I slipped off into the water. The surfboard popped up and smacked me in the head. I could hear this ringing sensation and felt the sting of the saltwater above my eyebrow, where the board cut me open.

I got back onto the board, paddled out to deeper water, and was pummeled by another wave. I saw Jessie, Lee, and Tommy at the shoreline. It looked like they were yelling at me, but I couldn't hear their voices over the roar of the ocean. I said to myself, "Come on, you can do this."

I paddled back out to try again. The swell caught my surfboard. I paddled faster, faster, and faster. I hopped up onto the board, trying to keep my balance. I closed my eyes, focusing on making my feet grip the wax on the board.

I opened my eyes inside the tube of the wave. I looked down and saw my feet firmly planted on the board.

I reached out with my hand and touched the water. I felt at one with the wave. I could feel its energy, and I was riding it, no it was better than that, I was a part of it. It was one of the most magical moments of my life. Looking through the water falling from the wave was like looking through a stained-glass window that God had created for me and no one else.

I wiped out shortly after coming out of the tube. When I came up for air, I heard Tommy yelling from the shore, "Ben! Sharks!"

Jessie and Lee joined him in yelling, "Sharks!"

I looked behind me to see a dark shadow approaching fast. I froze. I watched helplessly as a fin broke the surface of the water. I have never been so unable to move. Tears welled as I was brought back to every National Geographic show I ever saw on sharks. I wondered what part of my body was going to be lost. Would it suck me under?

It was only a few feet away, I grimaced. The water broke, as it came at me. A dolphin jumped over me. Then it came back. It came right up to me. I slowly reached out, and it moved its head to meet my hand. I placed my hand on its head and gently pet the dolphin. It looked at me with a smile, of course, they always look like they are smiling. Its skin was slick and soft but not slimy at all. Then other dolphins joined in. Now I wanted to stay another day. I wanted more of this moment. But isn't that true about all blessings in life?

The others grabbed their boards and paddled out. We all played in the water with the dolphins, laughing and having a blast. I thought about what Lee said, death is the mother of beauty. I wondered if this moment would have meant anything if it was in some pool in a Hawaiian hotel? Or was it meaningful because of the sacrifices we all made to get to this moment?

***

We were all laughing, sitting at a table in a local taco shack. It was mostly outside with rusted metal corrugated roof supported by two by fours with bamboo glued to them to make it look touristy. This was the first time I tried fish tacos, and they were pretty damn good until the heat hit.

"Dude, that was fly!" Tommy said.

"I'll never forget it!" Jessie said.

Lee smiled and said, "This is the best."

"Water, I need water!" Lee handed me his water, but it actually made it worse.

Tommy put up his hand, and we high fived, "Yeah, you did it!" he said. I really didn't care about anything but the fire that kept escalating in my mouth. Especially since it was now traveling down my throat.

"Milk works better for the heat. Jessie said, “Water makes it worse." I nodded and looked for the waitress.

Thank God, the waitress was already headed back to the table. She set my dad's card in front of me and said, "Excuse me. Permítame señor, but the card no work."

They all looked at each other, like crap now what?

I had my uncle's stash and knew we should be fine. All I wanted was some milk.

"Hold on," Lee said, "We have money in the car." The waitress nodded and left. How did he know about that money, I thought to myself?

"Guess it's time to go home," Tommy said. Why was everyone suddenly wanting to go home, I wanted to stay at least one more day.

We saw a rough-looking chef talking to the waitress, and he was making mean looking faces at us.

"Run!" Lee yelled.

They bolted from the table. I was like wait let's just pay them. The chef saw them running out and picked up a large knife. That signaled me to get up and run like the others. By the time I got out, they already were in the bus and had it started.

"Hurry up!" Lee yelled, "he's almost here."

"Go! Go! Go!" Tommy and I yelled.

I know Jessie was flooring it, but the bus moved off so slow. The chef was yelling at us in Spanish while running alongside the bus for a few moments, then we finally picked up enough speed to pull away from him. I guess Lee didn't know about my Uncle John's stash.

Chapter 16

The Snow Man

The driveway was empty, and the lights were off as we pulled into Lee's driveway. I don't remember how we got past the border, the ride back, or being in the bus and arriving at Lee's house at all, it's like my mind erased that stuff, it was missing from my journal too. I don't even remember entering the house. But I remember being there. I distinctly remember standing in the doorway paralyzed.

Vern held the passive body of Lee's mom, Wanda, by the scruff of her shirt with one hand. With the other, he brutally smacked her over and over again. The noises from the submissive cries, the pounding of flesh upon flesh, the static of the television noise, and the ticking of the grandfather clock mixed into a symphony of total discord.

Lee seemed emotionless about it, but when Vern glared at me in a threatening manner, a protective look came over Lee's face. Lee pulled out the Colt Cobra we had got from Trejo and pointed it at Vern.

Lee's hands shook as he said, "Leave us alone!"

Vern smiled at him and said, "Now look at that. The big man." He let go of Wanda and she fell to the floor like a lead doll.

"Go ahead, you little shit," Vern said, "take the shot. Come on! Shoot me! You yellow-bellied chicken shit!" Vern methodically moved to Lee, each step like a chess move.

Lee squeaked out, "Just..."

"Just what?" Vern asked. "Come on, you punk, do it. Prove you're a man. Pull the damn trigger."

The sweat was beading up all around Lee's face, he yelled at Vern, "I'll do it! I swear I'll do it!"

"Quit wasting valuable fucking air others could be breathing!" The back of Vern's hand landed squarely in the middle of Lee's face. Blood splattered all over. Lee's body went limp, falling to the floor.

The thud of Lee's body set into motion the sound of metal grinding on wood. The sound of grinding intensified as Vern picked up Lee and hit him again. I gazed down. For a moment, the world became surreal. I picked it up, the cold wooden handle with steel inlay set comfortably in my hand. It was heavier than I had remembered. I could see the bullets in it. It was so enchanting; my eyes were drawn to the mirror-like shine of the round wheel. Lee's body reflected multiple times along the round part that held the bullets in place.

I pulled back the hammer. The click of the hammer alerted Vern to my position. He tossed Lee aside and approached me much more cautiously than he did Lee. It was like he knew if he came at me, I wouldn't hesitate, would not waste a second. I would pull the *damn trigger.*

"How about you put that down." Vern took a slow step to me, and my body stiffened.

"Leave," I said. Stale mated, I could tell Vern wanted to rush, but instead treated me like a coiled snake keeping his distanced as he assessed my resolve. My heart pounded all the way up into my throat. Sweat burnt as it slid down the cut above my eyebrow into my eyes. Even with all the burning I felt, I refused to blink. Vern didn't blink either. He just slowly reached one hand behind his back. It looked like he was gripping something.

"I mean it," I said, "Leave now!"

"That's not happing." We were locked in a second of time.

Tommy and Jessie pushed their way into the room. Vern's body made an aggressive move, and my finger pulled the trigger. Vern jolted back but continued after me. I depressed the trigger again. He grabbed my shoulders with his strong boney hands. Face to face, I pulled the trigger again. His eyes locked with mine. It was like he could see right into my very soul. His eyes didn't close, they seemed to fade in intensity. A slight smile grew on his face before he fell at my feet.

I stood and stared at the blood, pooling around him. Time and reality returned to me. Instantly, the weight of what I had done was suffocating me. I lifted my chin, and they were all looking at me.

"OH my God!" Lee said. Sirens mixed with the ringing in my ears from the gunfire. "Get out of here!" Lee yelled.

I fixated on all the blood. The room came alive with commotion. Lee's mom ran off to who knows where, but I stayed there aloof.

"Come on, hurry up. I mean it!" Lee motioned to Tommy and Jessie, and they grabbed me hurrying me out, but when I got to the bottom of the steps, I halted the rushing.

"Wait! I can't leave," I said.

Lee grabbed the gun from me and said, "I got this. You save me, I save you. Now go!" Lee yelled.

"I can't," I said, "I can't let you take the –"

"Go!"

"I won't! You didn't do it!" I yelled. There was no way I was letting Lee retake the blame for something he didn't do.

"Ben, please," Lee pleated, "Trust me, you wouldn't last a day in juvie. Now get the hell out of here! Tommy, get him out of here."

Tommy nodded at Lee, grabbed his hand, and hugged him before ushering me off like Michael Corleone from the *Godfather*. Sirens continued to intensify with the ringing in my ears from the gunfire. I was conflicted, a part of me knew Lee was right, but I didn't want to pile on another lie.

Tommy and Jessie shoved me into the bus and slammed the door.

***

I sat at the same table I spun the credit card on just a few weeks before. I remember putting the card in the center of the table in front of my mom and dad. The house felt warm, the lights soft, it was such a contrast to Lee's home. I can definitely remember the ringing, the ringing sound from the gunshot was still present in my head. But no matter how hard I try, I can't recollect how I got home and how I ended up at the kitchen table talking to my parents. And even those memories seem more like scattered pictures.

I know I explained what happened. I can still see images in my head of my parents talking, but there's no sound from their dialogue. The only sounds I can recall were from the house, the kind of sounds that feel warm and welcoming.

And the fish tank, I still remember hearing the sounds from the fish tank.

My mom and dad looked more concerned than angry. I know for a fact I confessed every little thing, but what I said, or what my parents said, is still a mystery to me. I do call to mind, surprisingly, that they didn't react at all like I imagined they would have.

Mom put her hand on mine ever so gently as we sat there at the table. Dad, well, he went from sitting and standing a lot, but then he sat next to me. His face was so comforting as his arms surrounded me. That's when the ringing in my ears finally stopped. I do remember that much clearly. I thought for sure they would have never forgiven me, but the love they demonstrated was deafening.

Dad picked me up right out of the chair as if I weighed nothing and carried me to the couch. Mom followed closely, rubbing ointment on the cut above my eye.

Dad sat down with me in his arms and rocked me back and forth ever so slightly. Mom sat next to us and stroked my hair. Tears streaming freely down all our cheeks.

***

My parents hired a high-priced lawyer and got Lee out of jail. It was one of my greatest moments seeing the police bring Lee out and un-cuff him. The cool thing was watching my mom embraced Lee as if he was her own.

Then this guy in a dark suit lead us away from Lee to a narrow hallway. Mom paused the man and turned back to Lee and said, "We'll be right back for you, honey, don't you worry."

Lee thanked her with another hug. And when she went to let go, Lee didn't. He clung to her so tightly.

Mom said, “I promise it will all be ok,” After hearing her calming words, he reluctantly let go.

We followed the guy to an open door that lead into a small room. Mom, Dad, the Lawyer, and I squeezed our way in and sat at this rinky-dink table. Two detectives sat across from us. One was dressed in a bad, dull blue cheap looking Miami Vice type suit with a light pink dress shirt and a pink and blue striped tie. And the other one looked like he had just got off the golf course with a coffee-stained blue button-down shirt. The table had a dingy yellow phone on it off to the corner.

Don’t ask me what the lawyer actually said, cause I had no clue. Everything that came out of his mouth was fast and sounded more like a different language altogether. I mostly remembered his pompousness and air of confidence in what he was saying, not necessarily the exact words.

It felt like we were in that box for days, but mom always refers to it as her worst hour. The phone on the table rang. The detective in the cheap suit picked up the phone and listened intently. He had this total look of disappointment, like his dreams of getting on the Miami Vice show were just crushed. The lawyer could see right through those guys, it was kind of cool and scary all at the same time.

“Vern is still alive,” The detective said. This sent cold chills up and down my spine. In fact, I still get chills today, thinking about it.

After that, the lawyer looked even more pompous if that was even possible. Mom and Dad looked at me, relieved. Mom hugged me so tight.

You would have thought I would have been as relieved as my parents and lawyer, but I wasn't. I wanted Vern to pay, and part of me wanted to be punished as well, but I was let off due to some technicality, and just like that, it was over.

By the end of summer, Tommy had moved to Chicago and Jessie to San

Diego. Tommy continued to write Jessie, even though he was in another part of the country. After a few years, it paid off when she agreed to marry him. Tommy did everything he could to support Jessie's dream of being a fighter pilot. In 1994, she was among the first females to graduate from flight school and allowed to see combat in Iraq. Tommy spent his time rearing their kids and making a truckload of money in surf wear.

Lee ended up staying at my house for several years. One day out of the blue, he up and joined the military. His life turned out to be the biggest surprise of us all. I don't think anyone could have predicted that he would have become a chaplain in the military and later, after a tour in Iraq, become a full-time pastor. He made it a point to write and encourage all of us. He said his greatest joy came from seeing us make our dreams happen.

I was accepted into Stanford Medical School, where I minored in creative writing. While doing my residency, I got a master’s in creative writing online. I loved writing, but I also shared in my parent's love for helping people overcome illnesses. After Obama Care and all the HIPPA crap, I gave up my practice. Medicine just wasn’t fun anymore, and I was tired of feeling like I couldn’t make a difference. I got a job at a local junior college where I teach creative writing, and I'm still working on that first novel. I have to admit, although I miss my practice a little, I do love teaching.

Oh, remember that girl Sally, I helped to pass biology? Well, we bumped into each other at Starbucks a few times. One day she gave me her number on that old scantron, and well, we've been together ever since.

Over the years, we always said we would get together again for a day in the waves. Unfortunately, that never happened until today.

Here we are, surfers sitting on our old boards, facing each other in a circle, on a calm ocean. I look to my right at Sally, who has come to love surfing as much as me, Then to Jessie, Tommy, and their five kids. I still can’t find the words, and all eyes are on me.

You see, Lee died last week in a convenience store robbery. He made himself a human shield for a baby girl and her mother. So typical of him, always protecting those that either couldn't protect themselves or didn't know how.

When we first met, Jessie thought her worth came from athletics. Tommy, from being popular, for me it was getting everyone else's approval. And Lee, Lee thought it came from a piece of metal. But in the end, we were all wrong. What made us valuable was the very thing we were most afraid of... our own uniqueness.

I finally found the words, "One of Lee's favorite poets wrote, '*Death is the mother of Beauty; hence from her, alone, shall come fulfillment to our dreams and our desires.*' One of Lee's greatest desires was for us to all get back together again. It looks like he finally did it.

He told me something when he first got out of the military that I have always held close to my heart. He said dude, he always said dude, it's not how good we are, but how good we are to others. That was his dream after his stay in the military. And that's the dream I think I want now more than ever. So, in his words, from the last time we spoke, go find your dream and then go work as hard as you can until that dream comes true."

www.ingramcontent.com/pod-product-compliance
Lightning Source LLC
Chambersburg PA
CBHW030625130626
46552CB00002B/714